She was so close.

Fletcher could hear the soft puff of Anna's breath as she blew on her tea. Last week he'd have draped his arm around her shoulders as they sat on the porch swing, but tonight he wasn't sure the gesture would be welcome. Something was wrong. He was afraid she'd remembered the misgiving that had caused her to write the note the day of her accident.

His stomach clenched when she said, "Let's talk about the wedding. For starters, I don't remember if I've made your suit yet."

"*Jah*," he answered, half choking on the word in his relief. "You made it and I feel pretty dapper in it, if I say so myself."

"How about my dress?"

"You planned a sister day to work on it."

"*Gut* to know. Now if I can only remember about you and about our relationship. I've been praying that my memory will return any moment now and all will become clear."

"*Jah*, any moment now, all will become clear," he repeated.

But what would happen once it did?

Carrie Lighte lives in Massachusetts, where her neighbors include several Mennonite farming families. She loves traveling and first learned about Amish culture when she visited Lancaster County, Pennsylvania, as a young girl. When she isn't writing or reading, she enjoys baking bread, playing word games and hiking, but her all-time favorite activity is bodyboarding with her loved ones when the surf's up at Coast Guard Beach on Cape Cod.

Books by Carrie Lighte

Love Inspired

Amish Country Courtships

Anna's Forgotten Fiancé

Carrie Lighte

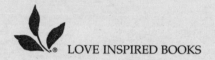 LOVE INSPIRED BOOKS

Recycling programs for this product may not exist in your area.

ISBN-13: 978-1-335-42799-1

Anna's Forgotten Fiancé

Copyright © 2018 by Carrie Lighte

All rights reserved. Except for use in any review, the reproduction or utilization of this work in whole or in part in any form by any electronic, mechanical or other means, now known or hereafter invented, including xerography, photocopying and recording, or in any information storage or retrieval system, is forbidden without the written permission of the editorial office, Love Inspired Books, 195 Broadway, New York, NY 10007 U.S.A.

This is a work of fiction. Names, characters, places and incidents are either the product of the author's imagination or are used fictitiously, and any resemblance to actual persons, living or dead, business establishments, events or locales is entirely coincidental.

This edition published by arrangement with Love Inspired Books.

® and TM are trademarks of Love Inspired Books, used under license. Trademarks indicated with ® are registered in the United States Patent and Trademark Office, the Canadian Intellectual Property Office and in other countries.

www.Harlequin.com

Printed in U.S.A.

Trust in the Lord with all thine heart; and lean not unto thine own understanding. In all thy ways acknowledge him, and he shall direct thy paths.
—*Proverbs* 3:5–6

For anyone who has ever suffered a
bumped head or a bruised heart,
as well as for those who have experienced
the healing power of love.

With special thanks to my agent, Pam Hopkins,
and my editor, Shana Asaro.

Chapter One

Anna Weaver slowly opened her eyes. Sunlight played off the white sheets and she quickly lowered her lids again, groaning. Her mind was swirling with questions but her mouth was too dry to form any words.

"Have a drink of water," a female voice beside her offered. "Little sips. Don't gulp it."

The young woman supported Anna's head until she'd swallowed her fill and then eased her back against the pillow. Anna squinted toward the figure.

"You've had an accident," she explained, as if sensing Anna's confusion. "You're at home recovering. It's your second day out of the hospital. How do you feel?"

"Like a horse kicked me in the head," Anna answered in a raspy voice. She blinked several times, trying to focus.

"You recognize me, don't you?" the woman asked. "I'm Melinda Roth, your cousin."

Technically, the woman wasn't Anna's cousin; she was her stepmother's niece. *I doubt I could ever forget the person who captured my boyfriend's heart*, Anna thought. Aloud she replied, "Of course I recognize you. Why wouldn't I?"

"The *Englisch* doctors said you still might have trouble with your memory, but apparently you don't," Melinda answered, appearing more disappointed than relieved.

Anna felt a pang of compassion. It was obvious Melinda felt guilty for what had transpired between her and Aaron. Anna had forgiven them both, but forgetting what happened was a little more difficult, especially since she had to live under the same roof—and share the same bedroom—with Melinda. Each time Melinda tiptoed into the room after her curfew, Anna was made acutely aware of how much her cousin was enjoying being courted by Aaron.

"The only trouble I have is that I'm a bit chilled," Anna said.

Melinda placed a hand on Anna's forehead. "You don't have a fever, thank the Lord. The doctor warned us to watch for that. I'll ask Eli to bring more wood inside for the stove."

"The woodstove in August?" Anna marveled. "That would be a first. Please don't trouble Eli on my account. I'm certain once I get up and move around, I'll be toasty warm."

"Lappich maedel!" Melinda tittered as she referred to Anna as a silly girl. "It isn't August. It's the first week in March."

Anna propped herself up on her elbows. Although she figured Melinda probably meant to be funny, her head was throbbing and she was in no mood for such foolishness. She knit her brows together and questioned, "You're teasing, right?"

Melinda shook her head and gestured toward the maple tree outside the window. "See? It doesn't have its leaves yet."

"How could that be?" A tear slid down Anna's cheek.

"Uh-oh, I've said too much." Melinda jumped to her feet and unfolded a second quilt over Anna's legs. "That should keep you warm."

Anna stared at her cousin, trying to make sense of the scenario. Then she began to giggle. "Oh, I understand! I'm dreaming!"

"Neh, neh," Melinda contradicted, giving Anna's skin a small pinch. "Feel that?"

Completely befuddled, Anna bent her arm across her face. First, she'd lost her boyfriend, then she'd lost her father, and now she feared she was losing her mind. It was simply too much to take in and she began to weep fully.

"You mustn't cry," Melinda cautioned. "The

doctor said it wasn't *gut* for you to become upset. We don't want to have to take you back to the hospital."

Melinda's warning was enough to silence Anna's weeping. "I don't understand how two seasons could have passed without my knowing." She sniffed.

"The doctors said it's the nature of a head injury like yours. You may remember things from long ago, but not more recently. You've also been on strong medications for your headache and for hurting your backside when you fell, so even your hospital stay might be fuzzy."

"It is," Anna acknowledged. "And I don't recall injuring myself. How did it happen?"

"You appear to have slipped on the bank by the creek, hitting your head on a rock," Melinda replied. "Do you know what you may have been doing there? Or where you were going? It was early Tuesday morning."

Anna tried to remember but her mind was as blank as the ceiling above. She shook her head and then grimaced from the motion.

"That's okay," Melinda said cheerfully. "How about telling me some of the more important events that you *do* remember?"

"My *daed*'s funeral," Anna responded. "It was raining—a deluge of water—and then the rain turned to sleet and then to ice."

She remembered because at the time she felt as if the unseasonably cold weather mirrored her emotions; a torrent of tears followed by a stark, frozen numbness that even the brightest sunshine couldn't thaw.

"*Jah*, your *daed* died a year ago. Last March. What do you remember after that?"

Anna thought hard. The days, weeks and months after her dad's sudden death from a heart attack were a blur to her even before her head injury. "I remember...your birthday party," she said brightly.

"My eighteenth. *Gut*. That was in late August. Do you remember when I got baptized last fall?"

It felt wrong to admit she couldn't recall Melinda making such an important commitment, but Anna said, "*Neh*. I'm sorry."

"That's alright. The doctor said your memory loss probably wouldn't last long, especially if you're at home, surrounded by familiar faces."

"Well then, if that's what it takes to cure me, I should get dressed and join the boys for breakfast," Anna stated, although she would have preferred a few more moments of rest before joining her four stepbrothers downstairs. She slowly swung her legs over the edge of the bed.

"They'll be glad to know you're well enough to rise," Melinda remarked. "But it's nearly time for supper, not breakfast. And the one who is most anxious to see you is your fiancé. He'll stop in after work again, no doubt."

"My fiancé?" Anna snorted. "But I broke up with Aaron after I caught you and him—I mean, Aaron is walking out with you now, isn't he?"

"Jah, jah," Melinda confirmed. Her cheeks were so red it appeared she was the one who had a fever. "You and Aaron broke up over a year ago. Last February, in fact." She hung her head as if ashamed, before looking Anna in the eye again and clarifying, "I was referring to your new suitor. That is, to your fiancé, Fletcher. Fletcher Chupp, Aaron's cousin from Ohio."

"Fletcher?" Anna sputtered incredulously. "I'm quite certain I'm not acquainted with— much less *engaged to*—anyone by that name."

Fletcher stooped to pick up a cordless drywall screw gun and a handful of screws that had fallen to the floor.

"Don't forget to gather all of your tools before leaving the work site for the evening," he reminded Roy and Raymond Keim, Anna's stepbrothers.

"We won't," Roy responded. "But those aren't ours—they're Aaron's. We didn't know if he was coming back or not, so we didn't dare to put them away."

"Where has he gone?" Fletcher inquired.

"Probably buying a soft drink at the fast-food place down the street," answered Raymond as he folded a ladder and leaned it carefully on its side along the wall.

Fletcher wished Aaron would set a better example of work habits for Raymond and Roy. He worried what their *Englisch* clients would think if they saw him taking numerous breaks or leaving early. Aaron's habits reflected on all of them. Although their projects had been plentiful over the winter due to an October tornado damaging many of the office buildings in their little town of Willow Creek, there was no guarantee that future contracts would be awarded to them, especially if their reputation suffered. Fletcher would need all the work he could get when he became a married man with a family to support. *That's* if *I become a married man*, he mentally corrected himself.

Nothing about his future with Anna was as certain as it had seemed when their wedding intentions were "published," or announced, in church on Sunday. Only two days later, on Tuesday morning, Raymond delivered a sealed note to him from Anna. *Fletcher,* it read, *I have a serious concern regarding A. that I must discuss privately with you before the wedding preparations go any further. Please visit me tonight after work. —Anna.*

The message was so unexpected and disturbing that if he hadn't been responsible for supervising Raymond and Roy, Fletcher would have left work immediately to speak with Anna. By the time he finally reached her home that evening, he was shocked to be greeted by a neighbor bearing additional alarming news: that morning Anna suffered a fall and was in the hospital. Although he loathed knowing she'd been hurt, he was simultaneously informed the doctors said she was going to be just fine. But it tormented him that he had no such assurance about the future of his relationship with her.

Each time he visited Anna, she was resting or couldn't be disturbed. Now, it was Friday and he still hadn't spoken to her. Ever since receiving her note, he'd felt as if he'd swallowed a handful of nails, and he'd barely eaten or slept all week. *Please, Lord, give me patience and peace, even as You provide Anna rest and recovery*, he prayed for the umpteenth time that day.

"I suppose Aaron's allowed to take breaks whenever he wants since he's the business owner's son," Roy commented, interrupting Fletcher's thoughts.

Although Fletcher agreed with the boy's observation, he chided, "Enough of that talk. My *onkel* Isaiah showed you special favor yourself in allowing me to apprentice you here, because your *mamm* was married to Anna's *daed* and he was such a skilled carpenter. Isaiah has been a *gut* employer to me, too. Regardless of how anyone else performs their work, *Gott* requires each of us to work heartily in whatever we do."

The boys finished tidying the site before stepping out into the nippy early-evening air. They wove through the rows of *Englisch* vehicles to the makeshift hitching post at the far end of the parking lot. Aaron's sleek courting buggy was nowhere to be seen as Fletcher, Raymond and Roy climbed into Fletcher's boxy carriage, given to him by his *groossdaadi*, or grandfather.

"Go ahead and take the reins," Fletcher said to Roy, the younger of the two teens. "It's important for you to learn to handle the horse during what the *Englisch* call 'rush hour' traffic."

As Roy cautiously navigated his way through the western, commercialized section of Willow Creek, Fletcher gave him instructive hints. He knew what it was like to lose your dad at a young age—and these boys had essentially lost *two* fathers; first, their own dad and then Anna's. He figured they needed all the guidance and support they could get.

"*Gut* job," he remarked when Roy finally made it through the maze of busy streets and down the main stretch of highway. From there, they exited onto the meandering country back roads that eventually led to the house Anna shared with her stepmother, Naomi, and Naomi's four sons, Raymond, Roy, Eli and Evan.

"Fletcher!" seven-year-old Evan whooped, sprinting across the yard when he spotted them coming down the lane. He tore alongside the buggy shouting, "Anna's awake!"

"Bobblemoul," eight-year-old Eli taunted, referring to his brother as a blabbermouth. He leaped down the porch steps after him. "You weren't supposed to tell. She said she isn't ready to see him yet."

"She said what?" Fletcher asked, hopping from the buggy after Roy brought it to a halt.

"Now who's repeating something they shouldn't?" Evan retorted to Eli.

"Roy, please hitch the horse for me," Fletcher requested and strode toward the porch, his heart hammering his ribs.

Naomi greeted him at the door with a wooden spoon in one hand and a bowl in the other. *"Kumme* in," she invited.

"Hello, Naomi. How are you?" he inquired politely before asking the question that was burning on his tongue.

"I'm *gut*," she said. "I see you're teaching Roy how to handle the horse in *Englisch* traffic? *Denki*—I worry about him around all those cars. He needs the practice."

"He's improving already," Fletcher remarked and then cut to the chase. "Is it true? Is Anna awake?"

"She is," Naomi replied. "But there's something you need to know."

"I've heard," Fletcher acknowledged. "Eli said she isn't ready to see me yet. I realize she probably needs a few minutes to get dressed and find her bearings. I can wait."

"Oh, dear," sighed Naomi. She sat down at the kitchen table and tapped a chair to indicate Fletcher should sit, as well. "I'm afraid that's not what she means by not being ready to see you. Do you recall the doctor said her memory might be impaired after the fall?"

Fletcher moved toward the table but he didn't sit, despite the heaviness in the core of his gut. He braced himself for another distressing disclosure. "*Jah*, I remember."

"Then you recall he instructed us it most likely would only be temporary, so there's no cause for alarm," Naomi continued cautiously. "However, before you see her, you should be aware she's having difficulty remembering anything at all that happened after late August or early September."

Fletcher gulped when he realized what Naomi was getting at. "I moved to Willow Creek in early September."

"Jah," confirmed Naomi, answering Fletcher's unasked question. "But the doctor said putting a face with a name may help her recollection. It's possible as soon as she sees you she will remember who you are. However, she might not. At least, not right away."

"Please, will you tell her I'd just like to see her?" he pleaded. "I haven't spoken to her since before her fall."

Naomi nodded. "I'll let her know and I'll ask Melinda to assist her down the stairs. Go through to the parlor. We'll give you two your privacy there. But, Fletcher, keep in mind she's been through a lot. She's very sensitive right now."

"I won't say anything to upset her," he promised.

As troubled as he was by Anna's last communication to him, Fletcher's primary concern at the moment was her well-being. Naomi had a tendency for excessive fretfulness; perhaps she was exaggerating the extent of Anna's memory loss? Pacing back and forth across the braided rug in front of the sofa, Fletcher wiped his palms on his trousers and bit his lower lip. The past few days without seeing Anna awake had seemed unbearably long, but this delay felt even more difficult to endure.

Someone cleared her throat behind him. He

turned as Anna made her way down the hall. Her honey-blond tresses, customarily combed into a neat bun, were loosely arranged at the nape of her neck, her fair skin was a shade paler than it normally was and she clutched a drab shawl to her shoulders, but she took his breath away all the same. Rendered both speechless and immobile with conflicting emotions, he choked back a gasp.

Her eyes were downcast, carefully watching her footing as she tentatively stepped into the room. He studied her heart-shaped lips and oval face, her slender nose and the tiny beauty mark on her left cheekbone. But it was the vast depth of her eyes, accentuated with a curl of lashes and gently arched brows, he yearned to behold. Fletcher and Anna had often conveyed a world of feeling with a single glance, and, in spite of everything, he hoped one glimpse into her eyes would convince him of her abiding love.

"Anna," he stated, moving to offer her his arm to help steady her gait.

She looked up and locked her eyes with his. Even in the dim glow cast by the oil lamp, he could appreciate their magnificent emerald green hue. She seemed to be searching his features, reading his expression, taking in his presence. He waited for what felt like an eternity, but his gaze was met by an impassive blankness.

"I've been told you're my fiancé, Fletcher," she finally said, although it sounded more like a question than a statement. His last wisp of hopefulness dissipated when she shook his outstretched hand, as if they were strangers meeting for the first time.

As Fletcher's expectant countenance crumbled into one of stark disappointment, Anna immediately regretted her gesture. What was she thinking, to shake his hand like the *Englisch* would? She wasn't working in the shop, introducing herself to a customer. She didn't understand why everything seemed so jumbled in her mind.

"I'm sorry, but I need to sit," she said and settled into a straight-backed chair, which made Fletcher frown all the more.

He perched on the edge of the sofa nearest her, leaning forward on his knees. His large, sky blue eyes, coupled with an unruly shock of dark hair, gave him a boyish appearance, but his straight nose and prominent brow and jawline were the marks of a more mature masculinity. She wondered how she could have forgotten knowing such a physically distinctive young man.

"I've been very concerned about you," he stated. "How are you feeling?"

"*Denki*, I'm doing better," she said, although

she had a dull headache. "Oh! But where are my manners? I should offer you something to drink. Would you like a cup of—"

She rose too quickly from her chair and the room wobbled. Fletcher again offered her his help, which she accepted this time, grasping his muscular forearm until the dizziness passed. Then he assisted her back into her seat.

"I didn't *kumme* here to drink *kaffi*, Anna," he said, crouching before her, still holding her hand. "I came here to see *you*."

Flustered by his scrutiny and the tenderness of his touch, she pulled her arm away and apologized. "I'm sorry I look so unkempt, but combing my hair makes my head ache."

He shook his head, insisting, "I wouldn't care if your hair were standing on end like a porcupine's quills, as long as I know you're alright."

Although she sensed his sentiment was earnest, her eyes smarted. Couldn't he see that she wasn't alright? And didn't he understand his nearness felt intrusive, given that she had absolutely no memory of him? He seemed so intense that she didn't want to offend him, but she wished he'd back away.

As if reading her thoughts, Fletcher retreated to his cushion on the sofa and said, "It's okay if you don't remember me yet, Anna. The doctor said this could happen. They told us your memories might return in bits and pieces."

Anna nodded and relaxed her shoulders. She hadn't realized how uptight she'd felt. She noticed his voice had a soothing quality. It was deep and warm, like her dad's was.

"Melinda told me a bit about you, but I have so many questions, I don't know where to start," she confessed.

"Why don't I give you the basics and if there's anything else you want to know, you can ask?" Fletcher questioned. When Anna nodded in agreement, he said, "Let's see—my name is Fletcher Josiah Chupp and I'm twenty-four. My *daed* was a carpenter. He and my *mamm* passed away by the time I was fifteen. I have three older sisters, all married, and sixteen nieces and nephews. I moved to Willow Creek, Pennsylvania, from Green Lake, Ohio, in September. My *onkel* Isaiah had been in dire need of another carpenter on his crew for some time."

"Because my *daed* died?"

Fletcher glanced down at his fingers, which he pressed into a steeple. "*Jah.* Your *daed* worked for Isaiah and he had a reputation among the *Englisch* of being an excellent carpenter. He left a big gap in my *onkel*'s business. No one could ever fill his shoes."

"No one could ever replace him as a *daed*, either," Anna murmured. After a pause, she asked, "So then, you live with your *ant* and *onkel*, and with Aaron and his sisters?"

"*Neh*. There wasn't room enough for me there. I live in my *groosdaaddi*'s home."

"Elmer! Your *groossdaadi* is Elmer Chupp! I remember him," Anna exclaimed. Then she realized aloud, "But of course I would, wouldn't I? I've known him for years. He was my *daed*'s first employer, before Isaiah took over their family business. You must greet him for me."

Fletcher rubbed his forehead. "I don't want to distress you, Anna, but my *groossdaadi* died in late December from pneumonia."

"*Neh!* Oh, *neh!*" Anna's bottom lip began to quiver.

"His passing was peaceful and it's a blessing to know he's not suffering the pain he endured toward the end," Fletcher said. "He always appreciated the soups and meals you made for him. And you were very consoling to me while I mourned."

"Dear Elmer Chupp." Anna clucked sorrowfully. "Didn't you say you lived with him?"

"*Jah*, I moved in with him when I first arrived in Pennsylvania," Fletcher clarified. "Now I live there alone. After you and I became betrothed, I discovered *Groossdaadi* willed his house to me, as his first grandson to tell the family of my intention to marry. For some reason, *Groossdaadi* chose not to follow the traditional Amish practice of bequeathing it to his youngest son, my *onkel* Isaiah. In any case, there were property taxes due, which you and I paid from my construction salary and your savings from working at Schrock's Shop, so the house is as *gut* as ours."

Anna's mind was reeling. She and Fletcher owned a house? On one hand, getting married and setting up her own household was a desire she'd harbored for years. On the other hand, with every new piece of information revealed to her, she was becoming increasingly uneasy at how seriously her life was intertwined with the life of a man who seemed like a virtual stranger, albeit, an appealingly thoughtful and stalwart one.

Pinching the bridge of her nose, she admitted, "I'm confused about the timing. In Willow Creek, it's customary for most Amish couples to keep their courtships as private as they can. They wait until July or August to tell their immediate families that they intend to marry. Their wedding intentions aren't published in church until October, and wedding season follows in November and December, after harvest. Yet Melinda says it's now March. Why did we already tell our families we intend to marry next fall?"

"We actually intend to marry next month,"

Fletcher responded. "You don't recall, but last October, Willow Creek was struck by a tornado. So many houses were damaged that Bishop Amos allowed those betrothed couples who needed to help their families rebuild to postpone their weddings until April. Of course, you and I were just getting to know each other last October, so we weren't yet engaged, but by January, we were certain we wanted to get married. We decided to take advantage of the bishop's special provision allowing for spring weddings this year."

"We only met in September and we're getting married in April?" Anna asked, unable to keep her voice from sounding incredulous. Six months was a brief courting period for any couple, and it seemed especially out of character for her. She had walked out with Aaron for over two years. As fondly as she dreamed of becoming a wife and a mother, lingering qualms had kept her from saying yes to Aaron's proposals, no matter how many times he asked. How was it she'd decided so quickly to marry Fletcher?

"Jah," he stated definitively. "As we confirmed to the deacon, we fully and unequivocally believe the Lord has provided us for each other."

Anna understood the implications. Prior to making their engagements public, Amish couples underwent a series of meetings with the deacon during which time the couple received counseling on the seriousness of entering into a marriage relationship. Although Anna had no recollection of those meetings, she knew if she and Fletcher completed the series and announced their intentions, it meant they were resolute about getting married.

"Have the wedding intentions been published in church?"

"They were announced on Sunday," Fletcher replied. "We'll be wed on Tuesday, April 7, five days before Easter and a week before Melinda and Aaron get married."

Anna inhaled sharply. "Melinda and Aaron are getting married?"

"Uh-oh," Fletcher said, smacking his forehead with his palm. "I assumed Melinda already told you."

"She probably didn't want to upset me."

Fletcher cocked his head. "Why would Melinda marrying Aaron upset you?"

"I d-don't know," Anna stammered. "I have no idea why I said that."

She was far more concerned about her own wedding than Melinda's. *I might as well be marrying the prince of England as this man, for as foreign as he is to me,* Anna thought, deeply disturbed. *Perhaps I should consider canceling our upcoming nuptials?*

"You were so excited after the intentions were published that you mailed the invitational letters to all of our out-of-town friends and family members first thing on Monday morning," Fletcher said. "Of course, the *leit* at church were invited and I extended several personal invitations on Monday evening, as well."

Upon hearing just how far their plans had progressed, Anna felt as overwhelmed by the prospect of calling off the wedding as she was by the prospect of carrying through with it. She silently prayed, *Please, Lord, if I really do know and love Fletcher Chupp and believe he's Your intended for me, help me to remember soon. If he isn't, please make me certain of that, too.*

Fletcher noticed Anna's face blanched at his words and he worried she might cry—or faint. "This must be a lot to take in," he said, trying to reassure himself as well as to console her. "The doctor said your physical well-being is the priority, and if you get enough rest your memories should take care of themselves."

Fletcher could always tell when Anna's smile was genuine because she had a small dimple in her right cheek. He saw no sign of it as she responded, "I can't imagine there will be much time for me to rest, with two weddings planned. I wonder how Naomi has been faring."

From his discussions with her, Fletcher knew how concerned Anna had been about her stepmother ever since Anna's father died. Naomi, who periodically suffered from immobilizing depression, was so grief stricken in the months following Conrad's death that Anna had almost single-handedly managed their household, with sporadic help from Melinda. In addition to caring for Eli and Evan, comforting Naomi and tending to the cooking, cleaning, laundering and gardening, Anna also worked at a shop in town so she could contribute to the household expenses. Her cheerful diligence was one of the qualities Fletcher most admired about her.

"I know you can't remember this," Fletcher said, "but Naomi began to regain some of her… her energy in January when you confided our decision to marry to her. You told me she embraced the distraction of planning for a wedding. She said it gave her something hopeful instead of dreadful to think about, and rather than wringing her hands, she could put them to *gut* use preparing for our guests."

"That sounds like the old Naomi, alright," Anna remarked and for the first time, her dimple puckered her cheek. But her smile faded almost as quickly as it appeared. "So then, if she is doing better, did I return to working at the shop full-time?"

During Naomi's period of bereavement, Anna reduced her working schedule from full time to part-time, much to the dismay of the shopkeeper, who valued Anna's skills. But as efficient as she was at assisting customers, Anna told Fletcher she drew more satisfaction from meeting her family's needs at home. She worked in the store only as much as was necessary to contribute to their living expenses.

"*Neh*, you're still only working there part-time."

A frown etched its way across Anna's forehead. "If I helped pay the property taxes for the house with my savings, and I've still only been working part-time, how has my family been managing financially? Furthermore, what will Naomi do when I move? Raymond's salary as an apprentice won't be enough to cover their expenses."

"*Jah*, you're right. That's why I asked my *onkel* to promote Raymond to a full-fledged crew member and to allow me to apprentice Roy. Raymond had already been satisfactorily apprenticed by your *daed* and there have been plenty of projects in the aftermath of the tornado, so Isaiah readily agreed. The arrangement has worked well for them and you've been happy that instead of needing to work full-time, you've been able to continue helping Naomi, er, recover, especially as you prepare the house for the weddings."

Averting her eyes toward the window, Anna responded in a faraway voice, "It sounds as if we've thoroughly addressed all of the essential details, then."

That's what I thought, too—until I received your message. Fletcher agonized, chewing the inside of his cheek to keep his emotions in check. He knew this wasn't the time to broach the subject, no matter how desperately he wanted Anna to allay his suspicions about her note.

"Supper's ready," Melinda announced from the doorway. "*Ant* Naomi says you're *wilkom* to join us, Fletcher."

"*Denki*, it smells *wunderbaar*, but I need to be on my way," he replied. As little as he'd eaten lately, Fletcher felt as if there were a cement block in his stomach and he doubted he could swallow even a morsel of bread.

As it was, Anna said she felt queasy and she wanted to go lie down.

"May I visit you tomorrow?" Fletcher asked before they parted.

"*Jah,*" she replied simply. Her voice sounded strained when she added, "*Denki* for coming by tonight," thus ending their visit on as formal of a note as it began.

Shaken by how drastically his relationship with Anna had changed within the span of a few days, Fletcher numbly ushered the horse along the winding roads leading to his home. Once there, he collected the mail from the box and entered the chilly house. He turned on the gas lamp hanging above the kitchen table to read his sister's familiar penmanship.

Dear Fletcher,
We were so joyful to receive word of the official date for your upcoming wedding that we got together to write you the very moment the letter arrived from Anna!

As your older sisters, permit us to say we knew how disappointed you were when Joyce Beiler abruptly called off your engagement, even though you tried to disguise the tremendous toll the breakup took on you. Ever since then, we have been faithfully praying that the Lord would heal your hurt and help your heart to love and trust another young woman again. We are grateful He answered our prayers for you so quickly in Willow Creek. It still puzzles us that Joyce chose to marry Frederick Wittmer, but we are grateful you have found a woman who truly recognizes what an honorable, responsible, Godly man you are.

Although our interaction with Anna was brief and we weren't yet aware you were courting, we were fond of her the moment we met her in Willow Creek in December. Even during such a somber time as Grandfather's funeral, she demonstrated a warmth and graciousness that lightened our burden. It is no wonder you are as committed to her as she is to you. Surely, your marriage will be blessed.

With love from your sisters,

Esther, Leah and Rebekah (& families)

Sighing heavily, Fletcher folded the letter and slid it back into its envelope. He understood the sentiments were well-intentioned. But under the circumstances, they opened old wounds of the nearly unbearable heartache and humiliation he suffered when Joyce canceled their wedding.

A single tear rolled down his cheek when he lamented how wrong his sisters were. Anna didn't even recognize his face, much less his character. While he didn't doubt her memory would return eventually, he was far less certain about her commitment to him. His sisters were right: the breakup with Joyce had nearly cost him his physical health and emotional well-being. He didn't think he could endure it if another fiancée called off their wedding.

He knew the message Anna had sent him by heart, but he picked up her note from the table where he'd left it that morning and held it to the light. *I have a serious concern regarding A. that I must discuss privately with you before the wedding preparations go any further.*

There was only one person she could have been referring to when she wrote "A."—Aaron, her former suitor. Fletcher shook his head at the thought. Even though his cousin had become romantically involved with Melinda, Fletcher long sensed Aaron was still in love with Anna. But once when Fletcher expressed his concern to Anna, she dismissed it out of hand.

"That's ridiculous. He broke up with me to court Melinda. She's the one he loves now," she argued. "Besides, you should know from all of our conversations that *I* haven't any feelings for *him* anymore. And whatever feelings I once had pale in comparison with how I feel about you. I may have liked Aaron, but I love—I'm *in* love with you, Fletcher Josiah Chupp."

On the surface, her response reminded him of the many conversations he'd had with Joyce, whom he suspected had developed a romantic affection for her brother-in-law's visiting cousin, Frederick. Joyce vehemently and consistently denied it, until four days before she and Fletcher were scheduled to wed, when she finally admitted the truth. But there was something fundamentally different about Anna, and as she declared her love for Fletcher, she stared into his eyes with such devotion that all of his worries melted away.

Fletcher remembered how, a few weeks after he and Anna confided their marriage intentions to their families, Melinda and Aaron announced they'd begun meeting with the deacon and they also planned to wed in the spring. Because Melinda seemed especially immature, their decision surprised Fletcher, but he was relieved to confirm Anna was right: Aaron was wholly committed to Melinda. Or so he'd thought at the time. But Anna's recent note shook his confidence to the core.

What in the world could have transpired concerning Aaron to make Anna hesitant to carry on with preparations to marry me? Burying his head in his hands, Fletcher shuddered to imagine. He knew from experience that people changed their minds. Engagements could be broken, even days before a wedding. There was still time. Was he was about to be forsaken by his fiancée for another man again? The possibility of having to withstand that kind of rejection a second time made Fletcher's skin bead with sweat.

The only way he'd know for certain was to talk to Anna about her note. But first, she'd have to remember what she meant when she'd penned it.

Chapter Two

As the sun began to light the room, Anna peered at her cousin asleep in the twin bed across from her. She rose to make the boys' breakfast, but when her feet touched the chilly floor, she pulled them back into bed, deciding to snuggle beneath the blankets just a little longer.

The tiny room on the third floor of the house was actually a part of the attic her father had sectioned off especially for her. More than once she'd knocked her head against the sloping ceiling and the room tended to be hotter in the summer and colder in the winter than the rest of the house, but she had always relished the privacy it afforded her from the four boys.

She'd had the room all to herself until Melinda's father sent Melinda to live with Anna's family a year ago in January because he wanted her to have better influences than he could provide. Naomi's sister had died twelve years earlier and her brother-in-law never remarried, so Melinda had grown up without any females in her home. It was said by many that she was capricious, or perhaps undisciplined. Some went so far as to call her lazy, a quality condemned by the Amish. Anna observed that the girl was generally willing to perform almost any chore, but she often became distracted in the middle of it and moved on to another endeavor.

"Half-done is far from done," was the Amish proverb Anna most often quoted to Melinda the first year of her residence with Anna's family. Serving as Melinda's role model had been a frustrating effort, yet Anna mused that if Melinda had committed herself to following God and had been baptized into the church, then her living with them had been worthwhile. It meant Melinda had put her wild *Rumspringa* years behind her; surely if she'd made that change, there was hope for other areas of her behavior, as well.

Melinda's eyes opened. *"Guder mariye."* She yawned. "I'm Melinda, your cousin."

Anna giggled. *"Jah*, I know. Are you going to introduce yourself to me every time I wake?"

Melinda laughed, too. "You were staring at me. I thought you didn't know who I was."

"I was marveling that such a young woman has decided upon marriage already."

Melinda sat straight up. "You remembered Aaron and I are getting married!"

"*Neh*, Fletcher mentioned it. He thought I already knew."

"Oh. Well, I'm not that young—I'm eighteen now. You're only four years older than I am," Melinda reasoned. "Besides, I've known Aaron over twice as long as you've known Fletcher. I think that makes us far better prepared to spend our lives together."

"Hmm," Anna hummed noncommittally. Melinda may have been eighteen, but at times she acted fourteen. Yet Anna couldn't deny she made a valid point about the brevity of Anna's relationship with Fletcher. Then she raised her hands to her cheeks as her cousin's words sank in—she herself was older than she remembered.

"That's right, I must be twenty-two now since my birthday was in September! Time flies when you have amnesia."

Melinda giggled and the two of them made their beds, got dressed and followed the smell of frying bacon down the stairs. When everyone was seated around the table, Raymond said grace, thanking the Lord especially for Anna's recovery. She was so hungry that she devoured as large a serving of food as her brothers did.

"If it's Saturday, that must mean you're working a half day today, right?" she asked Raymond and Roy, who both nodded since their mouths were full. "I can drop you off on my way to the shop. Joseph Schrock will be relieved to have me back."

"Neh," Naomi answered. "The doctor said you couldn't return to work until after your follow-up appointment. In fact, he said you should limit activities of exertion and anything that requires close concentration, such as sewing or reading, until he sees you again."

"Nonsense," Anna argued. "I'm as healthy as a horse—physically, anyway. There's no reason I can't ring up purchases and help *Englisch* customers decide which quilt to purchase or whether their grandchildren might prefer rocking horses or wooden trains. Besides, we need the income and Joseph needs the help."

Naomi began twisting her hands. "You have a doctor's appointment on Wednesday. Please, won't you wait until you receive his approval before returning to the shop?"

Not wishing to cause Naomi any undue anxiety, Anna conceded. "Alright, I'll wait. But you must at least allow me to help with the housework. How about if I prepare an easy dinner?"

"That sounds *gut,*" Melinda interjected. "If I drop the boys off at the work site before I go to the market, I'm certain Fletcher or Aaron will give them a ride home. Perhaps we can invite them for dinner, since Fletcher wanted to check in on Anna again today anyway?"

Anna caught Naomi's eye and gave a slight shrug. Melinda's habit of finagling a way out of chores in order to spend time with Aaron predated Anna's accident and she remembered her cousin's tactics well.

"Jah," Naomi permitted. "They're both *wilkom* to eat dinner with us. But I'll drop the boys off and go to the market myself. You may begin the housework and assist Anna in the kitchen if she requires it. Evan and Eli have yard and stable chores to complete."

Although Anna made a simple green bean and ham casserole for lunch, with apple dumplings for dessert, it took her twice as long as usual and she was grateful when Naomi suggested that she rest before everyone arrived. She felt as if her head had barely touched the pillow when Melinda wiggled her arm to wake her again. She disappeared before Anna could ask for help fixing her hair, because it still pained her head when she attempted to fasten her tresses into a bun. She winced as she pulled her hair back the best she could and pinned on her *kapp*.

"Guder nammidaag, Anna," Fletcher said when he crossed the threshold to the parlor. Warmth flickered along her spine as she took in his athletic, lanky build and shiny dark mane,

but she wasn't flooded with the rush of additional memories she'd been praying to experience at the sight of him. "How are you feeling today?" he asked.

"I'm fine, *denki*," she answered. Standing rigidly before him, trying to think of something to say that didn't sound so punctilious, she impulsively jested, "You're Aaron, right?"

Fletcher looked as if a horse had stepped on his foot. *"Neh!"* he exclaimed. "I'm Fletcher. Fletcher Chupp, your fiancé. Aaron is my cousin."

"I'm teasing!" she assured him, instantly regretting her joke. "I know who you are."

"You do?" he asked, raising his brows. "Your memory has returned?"

"Oh dear, *neh*," she replied. "I mean, I remember you from last night. I know that you're my fiancé. But *neh*, I don't remember anything other than that."

For a second time, he grimaced as if in pain, and Anna ruefully fidgeted with her *kapp* strings, wary of saying anything more for fear of disheartening him further.

"Naomi and Melinda are putting dinner on the table," someone said from the doorway.

When Fletcher moved aside, Anna spotted the familiar brunette hair, ruddy complexion and puckish grin. Although the young man bore a slight family resemblance to Fletcher, he was shorter, with a burly physique.

"Aaron!" she squealed, delighted to have recognized another person from the past, even if it was someone who'd brought her considerable heartache.

"I'm happy to see you, too, Anna," he replied before leading them into the kitchen.

Because there were two extra people, everyone had to squeeze together to fit around the table and Anna kept her elbows tightly to her side to avoid knocking into Fletcher, whose stature was greater than the other young men's.

"You made my favorite dish," Aaron declared appreciatively after grace had been said and everyone was served.

"Did I?" She didn't remember Aaron liking this casserole in particular.

"Don't pay any attention to him," Melinda piped up. "He says every dish is his favorite so the hostess will serve him the biggest helping."

Anna thought that sounded more like the jokester Aaron she remembered.

"Don't scare me like that," she scolded. "I panicked my memory loss was getting worse."

"Sorry, I didn't mean to," Aaron apologized. "But honestly, this casserole is Fletcher's favorite dish. Right, cousin?"

Without warning, Fletcher spat the mouthful

of noodles he'd been chewing onto his plate and guzzled down his water. Scarlet splotches dotted his face and neck.

"Does this have mushrooms in it?" he sputtered.

"Cream of mushroom soup, *jah*," Anna answered, appalled by his lack of manners. "I didn't realize you don't like them."

"I'm *allergic* to them!" Fletcher wheezed.

"Quick, bring me the antihistamine we use for Evan's bee sting allergy," Anna directed Melinda, who darted to the cupboard and produced the bottle.

Anna poured a spoonful of syrupy pink liquid, which she thrust toward Fletcher's lips. After he swallowed it, she gave him a second dose.

"Perhaps Raymond should run to the phone shanty and dial 9-1-1," Naomi suggested.

"*Neh*, the redness is starting to fade," Anna observed.

Indeed, Fletcher's breathing was beginning to normalize and within a few more minutes, his heart rate slowed to a more regular pace. Anna, Melinda and Naomi encircled his chair while the boys remained motionless in their seats, too stunned to move. Aaron nervously jabbed at his noodles with a fork, but didn't lift them to his mouth.

Fletcher coughed. "I feel quite a bit better now. Please, sit back down and eat your meal, if you still can after my unappetizing display. I'm sorry about that."

"I'm the one who is sorry, Fletcher." Anna's voice warbled and her eyes teared up. "I didn't know you were allergic. I could have killed you!"

"That's one way to get out of marrying him," Aaron gibed, reaching for the pepper.

"Aaron Chupp, what a horrible thing to say! Anna didn't do it on purpose," Melinda admonished, swatting at him with a pot holder in mock consternation as Anna fled the room.

"It was only a joke," he objected contritely. "No need to be so sensitive."

Fletcher pushed back his chair. "If you'll excuse me, a little fresh air always helps me feel as if I can breathe better after one of these episodes."

He stalked across the backyard, stopping beneath the maple tree. Inhaling deeply, he took a mental inventory of his grievances. First, Anna pretended she thought he was Aaron and then when Aaron actually entered the room, she seemed more delighted to see him than she'd been to see Fletcher. Second, he felt slighted by how carefully Anna avoided his touch. Of course, spitting his food out at the table—even if it was necessary—wasn't likely going to cause her to draw nearer to him anytime soon. But most irksome of all was Aaron's jape, *That's one way to get out of marrying him.* Was that just another one of his cousin's goofy attempts at humor, or did the joke have a more weighty meaning?

Fletcher picked up a stone and threw it as hard as he could in the direction of a wheelbarrow across the yard. With all of his might, he pitched another and another.

"*Gut* aim," Naomi said after each rock had clattered against the metal and he was empty-handed again.

"I didn't know you were behind me," he answered, embarrassed she'd seen his temperamental behavior.

"I wanted to be certain you were okay. Whenever Evan gets stung, the effects of the adrenaline linger for him, too. He says he has the most irritable thoughts, claiming it's as if the bees are buzzing around in his brain as well as under his skin."

"I don't know if I can blame my thoughts on adrenaline," Fletcher replied.

"Sometimes, we're not quite ourselves when we're ill or upset. Not Evan. Not you. Not me. Not Anna," Naomi said pointedly. "You have to give it time. Things will work out."

Naomi Weaver's gentle way of imparting wisdom reminded him of his own mother. *"Jah,"* he answered. "I understand."

"Gut. Now *kumme* inside for dessert."

Melinda was placing fresh bowls on the table, where the boys sat in silence. Anna had returned to the kitchen and was preparing dessert at the counter with her back to the others.

"Since I didn't eat any dinner, I should be allowed two helpings of dessert, don't you think?" Fletcher questioned Evan, tousling the boy's hair to break the tension in the room.

"How do you know if you'll like it, when you don't know what it is?" Evan asked.

"Well," Fletcher said, winking at him as Anna turned with a tray, "I've got high hopes it's molasses and mushroom pie."

Anna paused before pushing her features into an expression of exaggerated dismay. "Oh, dear! I've made the wrong thing—I thought mushroom *dumplings* were your favorite."

Fletcher clutched his sides, laughing. Now *this* was more like the kind of interactions he and Anna usually shared. Hilarity filled the room and when it quieted, Anna announced, "I am truly sorry for my mistake, Fletcher. I meant you no harm."

"There's no need to apologize—I'm the one who should have reminded you."

"Do you have any other allergies I should know about?"

"Just mushrooms," he stated.

"Gut." Then she addressed everyone. "What else has happened around here since early September? *Gut* or bad, I want to know. I *need* to know. It may help my memory *kumme* back. Also, I'd prefer that no one outside of this room, with the exception of the Chupp family, finds out I have my amnesia. In order to ensure that, I'll need to be made aware of what's been going on in Willow Creek."

"Grace Zook had a *bobbel*—a girl named Serenity—in January," Naomi told her.

"How *wunderbaar*!" Anna's fondness of babies was reflected in her tone.

Melinda added, "Doris Hooley married John Plank last fall, shortly after the tornado."

"Was anyone from Willow Creek hurt in the storm?" Anna asked.

"Neh, not seriously, although many houses and offices needed repair," Naomi said.

"Jah, the tornado was *gut* for business. For a while, we couldn't keep up with the demand. So I took over as foreman for my *daed*'s Willow Creek clients in May," Aaron stated. "He's handling the Highland Springs clients. They were hard hit, too."

Anna raised her brows and Fletcher wondered whether her expression indicated she was dubious or impressed to hear about Aaron's promotion to foreman. She extended her congratulations.

"We lost a beloved family member," Evan reported, his lower lip protruding. "Timothy."

Anna gasped. "Who is Timothy?"

"He was my turtle. I found him at the creek in October. His foot was injured from a fishing hook and I was caring for him until he was well again."

"That's very sad he died," Anna said, her mouth pulling at the corners.

"He didn't die," Evan clarified. "We lost him. *You* lost him. You were supposed to be watching him in the yard after church when it was our Sunday to host, but he crawled off. How could that happen? Turtles are naturally slow on land—and he was injured."

It happened because she wasn't watching the turtle, Fletcher reminisced as wistfulness twisted in his chest. *She was with me behind the maple tree and we were sharing our first kiss.*

"I'm sorry but I don't remember anything about that," Anna said and it took Fletcher a moment to realize she was speaking to Evan, not him. "How about if you, Fletcher, Eli and I take a walk to the creek to see if he has returned for the spring? Just let me do the dishes first."

"I'll do the dishes," Naomi insisted. "You ought not to touch any mushroom leftovers, lest your hands *kumme* into contact with Fletcher and he suffers another allergic reaction."

But there was little danger of that. Despite the temporary connection he'd just shared with Anna, Fletcher noticed she stayed closer to Eli and Evan than she did to him as they strolled down the hill, through the field and along the creek. Fletcher knew Anna's amnesia prevented her from recalling they rarely walked anywhere together without interlocking their fingers, but he felt too tentative about their relationship now to take her hand.

This early in March, they failed to spot any turtles, with or without injured feet. Once they returned home, Anna thanked Fletcher for his visit. Before leaving, he arranged to call on her the next day after dinner.

"Perhaps by then I'll be able to remember what your favorite dessert really is," she jested. "Although I suppose once my memory returns, we'll have more serious concerns to discuss."

"No doubt," Fletcher agreed as anxiety surged within him at the mention of "serious concerns," the same phrase she'd used in her note. Speaking to himself as much as to her, he added, "I guess we'll just have to wait and see what tomorrow brings."

* * *

"You look a little peaked," Naomi said when Anna entered the parlor where she was sewing. She folded the material into a square and stowed it in her basket.

"The glare of the sun bothered my eyes," Anna admitted. "And I feel a bit nauseated."

"Uh-oh, the doctor told us to let him know if you became sick to your stomach."

"I wasn't sick, just nauseated. But I don't think it's from my head injury," Anna rationalized. "It's probably because I ate too much too soon after going without."

"Kumme." Naomi extended her hand. "Take a little nap in my room. That way, you needn't climb the stairs."

"But I've been so lazy. I've hardly helped with a thing today."

"And well you shouldn't—I keep telling you that. Now go lie down on my bed and I'll fix us a cup of ginger tea. That should settle your stomach."

Anna removed her shoes and reclined on the side of the bed her *daed* had always slept on. His dog-eared Bible still lay on the nightstand. She picked it up and tried to read the print in German, but she felt too woozy to focus. Squeezing her eyes, she imagined her father poring over Scripture whenever he had a free moment toward the end of the day. She lifted the Bible to her nose, hoping to smell the honey and oatmeal scent of the salve he used on his cracked, calloused hands in winter, but she couldn't.

"I used to keep your *daed*'s sweatiest shirt hidden in my drawer so I could smell it whenever I missed him," Naomi said when she came in and saw Anna sniffing the Bible.

"Used to?"

"After a while, it stopped smelling like him and just smelled musty," Naomi reflected. "And I was ready to let the shirt go, because my memories of him are more tangible and comforting to me now. As the saying goes, 'A happy memory never wears out.'"

Bursting into tears, Anna placed her cup on the nightstand so she wouldn't spill her tea.

"Oh, Anna." Naomi sighed. "I'm so thoughtless. I shouldn't have mentioned my memories when you're struggling so hard to recall your own."

"*Neh*, it's fine, truly. I'm relieved to know you've been doing a bit better, Naomi. I wanted to ask, I just didn't know how to talk about… about your grief."

"Your faithful prayers and your quiet strength, along with all of your hard work, have kept our household going, Anna. I'm grateful for all you've done, even if it seemed I was too sorrowful to notice." Naomi squeezed her hand. "You remind me so much of your *daed*. I'll miss having you here every day, but I'm grateful *Gott* provided you such a *gut* man as Fletcher."

"Is he such a *gut* man?" Anna wondered aloud. "How do you know?"

Naomi blew on her tea before responding. "I suppose I don't know for certain. You and Fletcher were very secretive about your courtship—even more than most Amish couples customarily are. But I have observed how sincerely considerate he is of me and how helpful he has been to Raymond and Roy at work. Beyond that, I trust your judgment. I know there must have been very sound reasons you decided to marry him."

"I want to believe that," Anna said. "But I honestly don't remember what they are."

"Give it time, it will *kumme*."

"But there's hardly any time left! Aaron courted me for two and a half years and I still wasn't sure whether to marry him. How was it I was certain I should marry Fletcher after knowing him for less than half a year? What if the reasons don't return to me within this next month?"

"We'll build that bridge when we *kumme* to the creek," Naomi responded with Anna's father's carpenter variation on the old saying, "We'll cross that bridge when we come to it."

The two of them shared a chuckle before Naomi continued, "Even if it takes a while longer for your memory to fully return, I'd suggest you wait to make any changes to your wedding plans until the last possible moment. After all, if you postpone the wedding now and your memory suddenly *kummes* back, you'll have to wait until autumn's wedding season to get married. That delay can seem like forever to a young couple in love! Plus, you've already invited all of your guests. And, if you and Fletcher don't marry in the spring, it's my understanding the house could possibly go to Aaron and Melinda, which hardly seems fair since the two of you have already paid the back taxes. But you needn't think about any of that today. Right now, rest is the best thing for you."

Feeling reassured, Anna dropped into a deep slumber until she woke to someone rapping at her door. It was Melinda, declaring, "*Guder mariye*. Time to get up, *schlofkopp*."

Noting her surroundings, Anna suddenly understood why her cousin referred to her as a sleepyhead. "I slept here all night? Where did Naomi sleep?"

"Upstairs, in your bed," grumbled Melinda. "When I came in after curfew, she lectured me about how I must guard my reputation, even though I'm soon to be wed. By the time she finished her spiel, I hardly got a wink of sleep, but she let you sleep in, since it's an off-Sunday."

Although she felt completely refreshed, Anna was just as happy that church wouldn't meet again until the following Sunday—she didn't feel prepared to field questions about her injury from the well-meaning *leit* of her district. After breakfast, the family read Scripture and prayed together. They followed their worship with a time of writing letters, individual Bible reading and doing jigsaw puzzles, but since Anna was prohibited from activities that required using close vision, Evan and Eli took turns reading aloud to her. Then, after a light dinner, the boys were permitted to engage in quiet outdoor leisure and games.

"What will you and Fletcher do when he visits today?" Melinda asked her.

Anna shrugged. "I have no idea what kinds of things we enjoy doing together. I suppose we'll take a walk and talk." She secretly just hoped to get to know him better.

"That sounds rather boring. Why don't you *kumme* out with Aaron and me?" Melinda suggested. "We're going for a ride to the location where Aaron plans to build our house later in the spring. It will be a tight squeeze in his buggy, but we can fit."

"Are you sure you won't mind if we accompany you?"

"Of course not. After all, think of how many times you and Aaron let me tag along on your outings," Melinda said.

Anna remembered. She'd intended to demonstrate how a young Amish woman ought to behave in social settings and she naively believed Aaron was being forbearing in allowing Melinda to join them: she didn't realize he was interested in Melinda romantically.

"Besides," Melinda chattered blithely, "Naomi won't fret about my reputation if I'm out with you."

Anna sighed. So that was the reason she was being invited. Still, it seemed she and Fletcher had an easier time conversing when there were more people around. "I'd like that," she said. "As long as Fletcher doesn't mind."

Because they'd been so discreet about their relationship, Anna and Fletcher usually favored spending any free time they had with each other instead of attending social events within their district, such as Sunday evening singings. They'd certainly never accompanied another couple on an outing before, so Fletcher was startled when Anna asked if he'd like to join Aaron and Melinda on a ride to see the property Aaron intended to buy. But, realizing Anna wouldn't have remembered their dislike of double dating, Fletcher deferred to her request. Besides, he was heartened by the fact Aaron was considering buying property—perhaps it meant he was as dedicated as ever to marrying Melinda, and Fletcher's concerns about him and Anna were for naught.

The afternoon was unseasonably sunny and warm, and the tips of the trees were beginning to show dots of green and red buds. As the two couples sped up and down the hills in Aaron's buggy, Anna kept marveling at the changes in the landscape. She noticed nearly every tree that was missing and each fence post that had been replaced after the October tornado. She seemed especially aghast to discover the schoolhouse was one of the buildings that had suffered the worst damage, but she was relieved to learn none of the children had been harmed.

"Now that you've had more rest and you've seen the destruction, surely you must remember the storm," Aaron suggested. "It was so violent that I couldn't forget it if I tried."

Anna shrugged. "I still have absolutely no recollection of anything that happened in the past six months, whether big or small, positive or negative."

"I guess that's *gut* news for you, huh, Fletcher?

Anna can't remember any of your faults," Aaron needled his cousin. "On the other hand, she probably can't remember why she agreed to marry you, either."

Fletcher's mouth burned with a sour taste but before he could respond, Anna abruptly shifted the subject, asking Melinda, "Where will the two of you live until Aaron has time to build a house?"

"With Naomi and the boys," she replied, clutching Aaron's arm as he rounded a corner. "It will be crowded but I'm trying to convince Naomi to temporarily move into the room in the attic so we can have her room downstairs."

From the corner of his eye, Fletcher caught Anna frowning. He usually felt as if he could read her expression as easily as the pages in a book, but today he couldn't tell if she was scowling because of Aaron's rambunctious driving, Melinda's gall in asking Naomi to take the attic room, or some other reason altogether. The uncertainty caused his mouth to sag, too.

"Here we are," Aaron announced as he swiftly brought the horse to a standstill. He made a sweeping motion with his hand to indicate the field to their right.

"The old Lantz homestead?" Fletcher asked.

The modest square of land on the corner of the Zooks' farm used to belong to Albert Lantz, who resided with his granddaughter, Hannah. After their home was flattened by the tornado, they chose not to rebuild because Hannah married a visiting cabinetmaker from Blue Hill, Ohio, and thus moved out of state. Her grandfather accompanied her, but first he sold his property back to the youngest generation of the Zook family, who now lived on the farm.

"Their old homestead and then some," Aaron boasted. "The Lantz plot was barely as big as a postage stamp. I'm in negotiations with Oliver Zook to purchase the acreage running all the way down the hill to the stream."

"Isn't it *wunderbaar*?" sang Melinda, spreading her arms and twirling across the grass.

"*Jah*, it's lovely," Anna answered, but Fletcher noticed how taut her neck and jaw muscles appeared. Was she jealous? Was she imagining herself, instead of Melinda, owning a house with Aaron in such a picturesque location? Fletcher stubbed his shoe on a root as the tumultuous thoughts rattled his concentration.

"*Kumme*, have a look at my stream," Aaron beckoned.

"I believe the stream belongs to *Gott*, although He's generous enough to allow it to run through your property—or actually, through Oliver Zook's property," Fletcher stated wryly.

"Lighten up. Worship services are over for

the day," Aaron countered. "Or if you're going to preach at me, how about remembering the commandment, *Thou shalt not covet*?"

"Stop bickering," Melinda called. "This is a happy occasion, remember? Hooray!"

She picked up a handful of old, dried leaves and tossed them into the air and then tried to catch them as they fluttered around her. Then she and Aaron cavorted down the hill like schoolchildren, racing to tag each other's shadows until they disappeared into the woods, while Fletcher and Anna followed at a slower pace, neither one speaking.

When they reached the stream, Anna closed her eyes and inhaled deeply. "Mmm, it smells like spring," she said, and then raised her lids to view the bubbling current, the gently sloping embankment and the thick stand of trees. "What a beautiful place."

"I have to agree, it's a fine fishing spot," Fletcher responded. Thinking aloud, he added, "But Aaron's too impatient to fish and even if he weren't, Melinda's such a chatterbox, she'd frighten the fish away."

Anna narrowed her brows. "That may be true of them now," she said, "but people change. They grow. With *Gott*'s help, we all do."

Fletcher hadn't intended to be insulting. He simply meant the location seemed better suited to his and Anna's preferences than to Aaron and Melinda's, since he enjoyed fishing and Anna appreciated solitude, so he was surprised by how quickly Anna seemed to defend them. And what did her comment about people changing and growing mean, anyway? Was she indicating that she had changed? Was she implying she thought Aaron had grown? Fletcher's brooding was interrupted when Melinda capered up the embankment.

"Help!" she squealed. "Aaron's trying to splash me and that water's freezing!"

Aaron reappeared and the four of them ascended the hill. At the top, they were greeted by Oliver Zook. "*Guder nammidaag.* Grace sent me to invite our prospective new neighbors and their future in-laws for cookies and cider."

"That sounds *wunderbaar*," Melinda said, accepting the invitation for all of them.

The fragrance of hot cider and freshly baked cookies wafted from the kitchen when Grace ushered everyone inside. As they situated themselves in the parlor, where Doris and John Plank were also visiting, the Zooks' baby began wailing in the next room.

"I'll get her while you prepare the refreshments," Oliver said, squeezing his wife's shoulder.

"Wait till you see how much she's grown

since the last time you saw her, Anna," Grace remarked before leaving the room, understandably ignorant of Anna's amnesia.

When Oliver returned, jostling the fussy baby, Aaron suggested, "You should let Anna take her. She has such a soothing, maternal touch. She was always able to comfort my eldest sister's son when he was a newborn."

"*Jah*, I remember," Anna said, smiling as she lifted Serenity from Oliver's arms. "Your nephew had colic and your poor sister was exhausted because he gave her no rest."

Although he knew it wasn't Anna's fault, Fletcher felt a slight twinge of sadness that she could remember everything that happened during her courtship with Aaron, but not a thing that happened during her courtship with him. And who was Aaron to openly flatter Anna, as if he were still her suitor? Of course, Aaron's compliment was well deserved: within a few moments of cooing and swaying, the *bobbel* had fallen asleep in Anna's arms. She sat back down and accepted a cup of cider from Grace with her free hand.

"See that, Fletcher? The *bobbel* in one hand, a cup in the other." Oliver laughed. "Anna will have no problem keeping your household in order."

Anna demurely glanced at Fletcher from beneath her lashes and a tickle of exhilaration caused his nerves to tingle. He momentarily forgot all about her note as a glimpse of their future *bobblin* flashed across his mind's eye.

"You're a fortunate man, indeed," Doris Plank interjected. "But I have to say, you could have knocked me over with a feather when the intentions were announced. For the longest time, I suspected Aaron was betrothed to Anna. Even after it was rumored he'd begun walking out with you, Melinda, I always assumed he'd eventually wind up with Anna again, don't ask me why. But then, I never expected I'd marry John, either, so I guess it's a *gut* thing I'm not a matchmaker!"

As Doris gleefully tittered at her own humor, Fletcher's ears burned and his jaw dropped. Doris had a reputation for making bold remarks, but he'd personally never been on the receiving end of one and he didn't know how to respond without sounding rude himself.

"*Jah*, life is full of *wunderbaar* surprises for everyone, isn't it?" Grace diplomatically cut in. She passed the tray to Anna. "Here, Anna, you haven't had a cookie."

"*Denki*, but *neh*," Anna declined. "I... I..."

"She has to watch her figure," Melinda finished for her. "But I don't, so I'll take some."

"Ah, you must have finished sewing your

wedding dress then, Anna?" Grace's eyes lit up. "You don't want to have to make any last-minute alterations, is that it? If you're anything like I was, you're counting down the days!"

Blushing, Anna gave a pinched smile and a slight shrug but didn't answer.

"You're fortunate your intended is so calm, Fletcher," Oliver remarked, as he patted his wife's hand. "As soon as our intentions were published, the wedding preparations were all Grace talked about to anyone who would listen. And even to some people who wouldn't!"

As everyone else laughed, Fletcher did his best not to frown, acutely aware that Anna's last communication about their wedding preparations had been anything but enthusiastic.

Suddenly, Melinda sniffed exaggeratedly and declared, "Oopsie! I think Serenity needs a diaper change."

All three couples soon made their way out the door. As they departed the farm and headed back toward Anna's house, Fletcher thought, *The* schtinke *of a dirty diaper makes a fitting end to this afternoon*. Disappointed that he and Anna hadn't exchanged a private word between them, and feeling even less certain about their future today than he'd felt all week, Fletcher decided the next time he went out with Anna, they were going out alone.

Chapter Three

The Sabbath was supposed to be a day of rest, but Anna felt utterly exhausted by the time she said her prayers and slipped into bed. Yet as achy and tired as her body was, her brain was wide-awake, reliving the afternoon's unpleasant events.

First, the buggy lurched about so much, she'd become increasingly nauseated as they journeyed toward their destination. Second, she was nettled by Aaron's wisecrack about her continued inability to remember Fletcher—and judging from Fletcher's expression, he was equally peeved. Third, Melinda's prancing and twirling caused Anna's head to spin. Then, Fletcher and Aaron squabbled like two boys on a playground. Finally, when she tried to focus her attention on something positive by commenting on the beauty of the scenery, Fletcher pulled a face.

His remarks about Aaron's and Melinda's personalities may have been true, but they weren't especially generous, which made her wonder if he was characteristically judgmental.

Not that Aaron or Melinda took much care to measure their own words about others: Melinda's pronounced insinuation that Anna needed to watch her weight would have been humiliating, had it been true. In reality, she'd been far too nauseated to eat any cookies, but she didn't want to draw attention to herself by saying so.

Of course, all eyes had been on her when Grace questioned Anna about whether she'd sewn her wedding dress or not. Making her dress was one of the wedding preparations an Amish bride reveled in most, but Anna couldn't even recall if she'd bought her fabric yet. Nor did she know if she'd selected her *newehockers*, also known as sidesitters or wedding attendants, and given them the fabric for their dresses, which would match hers. Had she made Fletcher's wedding suit for him, as was the tradition?

If she hadn't begun sewing yet, should she bother starting now, given that her memory might not return in time to carry through with the wedding? On the other hand, if she delayed making the garments until her memory returned, it was likely she'd have to rush to finish them, since there were only a few weeks until the wedding as it was.

Of course, her dilemma about their wedding clothes wasn't nearly as disconcerting as her growing concern about whether or not they should get married at all. Anna hesitated to bring up the subject with Fletcher, who demonstrated no signs of hesitation about carrying through with their plans. Considering all they'd apparently invested in their relationship, their house and their wedding, how could she tell him she had doubts about their future together? Once her misgivings were voiced, there'd be no taking them back. Even if her concerns were legitimate under the circumstances, Anna was aware of how deeply they might hurt Fletcher. Completely exasperated, she cried herself to sleep, stirring only once when Melinda's footsteps creaked on the stairs.

By morning, she resolved to exercise more patience as she waited upon the Lord to guide her about what to do next in regard to the wedding. After praying once again for her memory to return—and for a sense of peace in the meantime—she managed to comb her hair into a loose likeness of a bun. She had breakfast on the stove before Naomi could forbid her to help. She knew her stepmother was only concerned for her health, but Anna was growing increasingly restless from being told she couldn't do her share of work around the house.

Naomi chided her anyway. "The doctor said for you to take it easy. Where is Melinda hiding this morning?"

"Here I am," Melinda answered, skittering into the room.

"*Gut.* Since you and Anna need the buggy to go into town today, I'll drop Raymond and Roy off at work," Naomi suggested. "While I'm gone, I'd like you to clean the breakfast dishes and wring and hang the laundry, please. And remember, Anna isn't to help with any housework until she's seen the doctor again."

The ride to the mercantile was much smoother than it had been in Aaron's buggy, and on the way, Anna asked Melinda about their shopping list. She assumed they were picking up grocery staples for the week and she thought dividing the list would make the task easier.

"Oopsie, you must have forgotten our plan, since we arranged today's outing prior to your accident," Melinda replied. "We're not buying groceries. I'm buying organdy for my wedding apron. I also need to check to see whether the fabric has arrived for my dress and my *newehockers*' dresses. Aaron's mother is sewing his wedding suit, so I needn't concern myself with that. What do you intend to purchase today?"

Anna swiveled toward her and cocked her head, racking her brain. If only Melinda had reminded her they were going fabric shopping, she might have had an opportunity to discuss the matter with Naomi, whose practical and Godly advice she valued.

"I don't know that I'll purchase anything," she finally responded. "After Grace's question yesterday, I checked my sewing basket and the closet this morning and I didn't find evidence I've been working on my wedding dress, but I didn't have a chance to ask Naomi if I might have hung it somewhere else. Nor do I know if I've finished Fletcher's suit. I don't even know whether I've chosen my *newehockers* or who they might be."

Melinda clicked her tongue. "That's the trouble with being so secretive. To be honest, it hurt my feelings a bit that you never confided in me about your relationship with Fletcher. Perhaps if you'd told me more, I'd be able to help determine your sewing needs now. But, as Aaron and I agree, it makes sense that you and Fletcher hid your courtship from everyone, especially from us."

Anna silently counted backward from ten before responding. "Plenty of Amish couples still practice discretion about sharing their court-ship—the custom isn't intended to insult anyone, so I'm sorry if you felt that way," she said. Taking a deep breath, she asked, "But what do you mean it made sense we'd keep our courtship hidden, especially from you?"

"Oh, you know," Melinda prattled on obliviously, working the reins. "I imagine you might have worried if you brought Fletcher around socially, he would have been drawn to me, the way Aaron was. Not that I'd ever be interested in Fletcher, of course, but you must have some lingering worries. It's only natural. Also, Aaron said the two of you never kept your courtship such a secret. He thinks that you and Fletcher didn't let anyone know you were courting because you were worried Aaron might tell Fletcher that he was your second choice."

"Oh really?" Anna asked drily. What hogwash! She was the one who begged her father and Naomi not to send Melinda back to Ohio after she discovered her shenanigans with Aaron! And she was the one who insisted she was glad Melinda had found an Amish boyfriend instead of an *Englischer* because maybe he'd be a good influence on her! As for Aaron, she'd gotten over their breakup within a couple of weeks. Some of his ideas were so preposterous Anna wondered why she'd ever accepted him as her suitor.

They continued in silence until they reached

the designated horse and buggy lot on the far end of Main Street. After they'd secured the animal at the hitching post, Anna said, "I'm going to Schrock's while you're at the mercantile. I expect you back within half an hour, please."

The bells jingled when she pushed open the door of Schrock's Shop, and Anna's agitation was replaced with a sense of nostalgia. She took special pleasure in the resourcefulness and creativity of the Amish *leit* from her district, who consigned their handiwork in the large store. Today the gallery bustled with tourists in search of specialty Amish items such as quilts, toys, furniture, dried flower wreaths and naturally scented candles. She knew Joseph Schrock must have been pleased so many people were making purchases, although he looked overwhelmed by the line stretching from the register to the door. It seemed such a shame Anna couldn't work that afternoon, but she decided not to add to Joseph's burden by interrupting him with small talk.

She browsed the aisles, noting the price and location of the inventory. *I don't recall any of these items being stacked here*, she thought. She took a square of paper and a pencil from her purse and jotted down the contents on the shelves so she could study them before returning to work. When she finished, she turned to leave, nearly bumping into another young Amish woman whose arms were loaded with bars of homemade soap.

"Excuse me," she apologized, bending to retrieve the bars that had spilled from the woman's grasp.

"Anna!" the woman declared. "It's so *gut* to see you—I wasn't sure if you'd be stopping in today. We've been praying for you since we heard about your head injury. How do you feel?"

Anna surveyed the woman's olive complexion, pronounced cheekbones and deep-set eyes. She couldn't register who she was, although she deduced the woman also worked in the store.

"I'm much better," she said slowly. "*Denki* for your prayers."

"Of course," the woman replied. "As you can see, there's a long line now, but if you give me fifteen minutes, I'll be able to take my break and we'll catch up on everything."

"Actually, I was just popping in for a moment. Will you kindly tell Joseph I'll return to work on Thursday if the doctor approves? I'm sorry, but I have someone waiting and I can't stay." Anna backed away before it became apparent she couldn't recall the woman's name.

On the way home, Melinda jabbered nonstop about how irritated she was because the particular shade of purple fabric she'd ordered for her wedding dress hadn't arrived yet. Anna didn't get a word in edgewise until they sat down for tea at home, where she told Melinda and Naomi about her puzzling interaction with the unfamiliar woman.

"She's clearly new to Willow Creek. She's about my height and has dark hair and a ready smile," Anna commented.

"It must have been Tessa, one of the Fisher sisters," Melinda guessed. "Was she a homely woman with a big nose?"

"Melinda!" Naomi snapped.

"What?" Melinda chafed. "I'm only giving an honest description of what she looks like. Doesn't *Gott* require us to be honest?"

"First, beauty is in the eye of the beholder, and second, *Gott* requires us to be kind," replied Naomi. "And in this house, so do I."

Anna seldom heard Naomi raise her voice like that and Melinda looked as surprised as Anna felt. The young woman snatched her coat from the hook and stomped outside.

After the door banged shut behind Melinda, Naomi confessed, "Even though she's my dear departed sister's *kind*, there are times when her churlish behavior tries my last nerve and I fear I don't have any patience left."

"She's young and she doesn't always weigh her words," Anna acknowledged, consoling herself as much as Naomi. "I suppose that's the result of not having a *mamm* or sister in her home for so many years and then running around with the *Englisch* as often as she did."

Naomi sighed. "'Tis true, I suppose. In any case, Tessa Fisher and her older sister, Katie, moved to Willow Creek together in the fall. They rent Turner King's *daadi haus*. Katie took Doris's teaching position when Doris got married. Tessa works at Schrock's. The three of you became fast friends—you've spent many sister days and Sunday visits at their house."

"No wonder she looked so perplexed," Anna said. "She must have thought me terribly rude not to even greet her by name."

"I'm certain she'll understand once you explain the reason. But even without having all the facts, a *gut* friend will always give another the benefit of the doubt."

"*Jah*, that's true," Anna agreed, sipping her tea. As she reflected on Naomi's words, Anna decided that although she didn't have all of the facts about Fletcher, she was going to try to be more open about giving him every benefit of the doubt, too. As her fiancé, he deserved that much.

"I'll take Roy and Raymond home," Aaron offered at the end of their workday.

"*Neh*, I gave Naomi my word I'd do it when I

saw her this morning," Fletcher countered. He had also been asked to stay for supper.

Aaron shrugged. "Suit yourself, but I'm going that way anyhow, since I'm picking up Melinda. She and my *mamm* and sisters are working on the wedding clothes together."

Fletcher was relieved Aaron and Melinda wouldn't be at the house. While he didn't expect to be able to spend much time alone with Anna, he was already on tenterhooks about his relationship with her; he didn't want to be harried by Aaron's snide remarks or Melinda's animated mannerisms. Besides, his appetite was beginning to return and he looked forward to eating another home-cooked meal instead of the soup and sandwich supper he usually prepared for himself.

After supper, he turned to Anna. "It's a clear night. Would you like to take a drive in the buggy or a stroll down to the creek?" he asked. "I'll bring a flashlight."

She hesitated. "How about if we sit on the porch instead? I'm afraid my energy is lagging. Would you like a cup of hot tea?"

"*Jah*, please," Fletcher answered.

They carried their steaming mugs out to the porch and peered over the railing, up at the starry sky, standing so close that Fletcher could hear the soft puff of Anna's breath as she pursed her lips to blow on her tea. A week ago, he would have draped his arm around her shoulders and nestled her to his chest, but tonight he had no assurance the gesture would be welcome, so he stepped away so as not to bump her with his elbow when he lifted his own mug to drink.

"I think spring might be coming early this year. Listen, you can hear the peepers," he said, indicating the chirping call of nearby frogs.

"Speaking of peepers, don't turn around," Anna instructed, glancing sidelong. "Evan is doing something he's expressly been forbidden to do—he's eavesdropping at the window. Ignore him. He can't hear us anyway."

Despite her admonishment not to look at him, Fletcher wheeled around and made a monstrous face to send Evan scampering, which sent Anna into a fit of giggles.

"Let's sit," she suggested, but no sooner had they settled into the swing next to one another than Anna got up and moved to the bench.

"Do I smell bad or is something else wrong?" he asked, suddenly fearful she'd remembered the misgiving that caused her to write the note the day of her accident.

"*Neh!* Of course not. I'm sorry, I should have explained… I've been so nauseated that even the rocking of the swing causes my stomach to flip. I haven't wanted to say anything because I didn't want to alarm anyone."

"Oh, I see," Fletcher said and his muscles immediately relaxed. So that was all it was. "Are you sure you shouldn't call the doctor?"

"*Neh*, I'm not sick," she assured him. "They told me I might temporarily have motion intolerance and I think I'm still recovering from Aaron's handling of the buggy yesterday. It seems lately I've been sensitive to certain smells and sights, too. And even though Melinda was the one twirling in circles yesterday, I felt as if I was the one becoming dizzy just from watching her."

"Is there anything I can do to help?" Fletcher asked.

"Don't twirl in circles," Anna quipped.

Fletcher chuckled heartily; Anna always could make him laugh. "I hope the bouts of nausea pass soon."

"*Denki*," Anna replied. "To be on the safe side, I'll mention it to the doctor when I see him on Wednesday, although I'm more interested in knowing when he thinks my memory will fully return. Meanwhile, it would be helpful if I could ask you a few questions."

"Of course," Fletcher agreed.

"Well, right now, my immediate concerns are actually about the wedding preparations."

Fletcher's hand trembled so noticeably he

had to set down his mug of tea. Squaring his shoulders as if to brace himself for whatever Anna was about to disclose, he could only utter, *"Jah?"*

"For starters, I don't know if I've made your suit yet. Do you?"

There was a pause while her question sank in and when it did, Fletcher was nearly woozy with relief. *"Jah,"* he answered, half coughing and half choking on the word. *"Jah,* you've already made my suit and I feel pretty dapper in it if I do say so myself."

"Oh, *gut."* Anna's teeth shone in the moonlight. "How about my wedding dress? Have I mentioned anything about that?"

"Only that you might plan a sister day to work on it, along with your *newehockers."*

"Have I told you who they are?"

"Katie and Tessa Fisher."

Anna exhaled. "It's so *gut* to know these things. Now I can get back to working on the preparations before too much time elapses and I fall behind with the things that need to be done. I mean, obviously, there's so much I want to remember about you and about our relationship, too, but I've been praying fervently that my memory will return any moment now and all will *kumme* clear in that regard."

"Jah, any moment now, all will *kumme* clear,"

Fletcher repeated. But what would happen once it did? A shiver made his shoulders twitch.

"Oh, you're cold," Anna observed. "We should go inside."

"Actually, it's getting late and I ought to head home." Fletcher felt drained from the gamut of emotions he'd just experienced. "Unless you have any other urgent questions for me?"

"Only one. Actually, it's more of a favor. As I mentioned, I have a doctor's appointment on Wednesday. It's all the way in Highland Springs and it's at three o'clock, the middle of your work-day. But I'm not supposed to take the buggy out until I've gotten the all-clear from the doctor and you know how nervous Naomi gets. I'd ask Melinda, but she isn't too careful on the major *Englisch* roadways... More important, I'd like you to be able to ask the doctor any questions you might have, too."

"Of course I'll take you," Fletcher agreed, although he very much doubted the doctor was the person who could give him the answers he most needed to know.

When Anna told Naomi about the plan for Fletcher to bring her to the medical center, Naomi seemed relieved not to have to take the buggy through city traffic.

"You promise you'll ask the doctor whether or not you're able to return to work?" she prodded.

"Of course I will," Anna reassured her. "What I'm more concerned about is helping you with preparations for the weddings."

"Don't worry about that," Naomi said, cupping Anna's face in her hands. "Having to prepare for the weddings was the best thing that could have happened to me. Without the deadline of your wedding dates, who knows how long I might have lolled about in misery?"

"I'm glad you're feeling more energetic, but I still intend to help. There's so much cooking, cleaning and organizing to do. And wherever will our guests stay?"

"I'll *wilkom* your help if the doctor allows, and for what it's worth, I intend to put Melinda to work, too. As for our guests, some of them will stay here and those who are related to the Chupps will stay with Aaron's family. We'll make do. I'm just pleased to hear you're more certain about going through with your wedding now."

Anna hardly felt certain, but Naomi was so upbeat that Anna didn't want to discourage her by rationalizing that even if she canceled her wedding to Fletcher, their household preparations wouldn't be in vain, since Melinda's wedding was only a week later. Instead, she replied,

"As you've said, there's still time to decide. And I'm hopeful the doctor will have something promising to say about when I can expect my memories will return."

The medical center was on the opposite end of Highland Springs and although Fletcher worked the horse into a fast clip, he took care to ensure the carriage remained steady. They arrived in plenty of time for Anna to check in and he dropped her off in front of the building so he could take the buggy around the corner to the designated lot. Aaron had rarely been heedful of her comfort, so Anna was pleasantly surprised by Fletcher's chivalry, especially in light of her anxiety about the appointment.

"Would you like me to *kumme* into the examining room with you?" Fletcher asked when he reunited with her in the waiting area.

"*Jah*, I think the doctor is only going to look into my eyes and talk to me about my progress. And this way, you can ask him your questions, too," she suggested. The truth was Fletcher's presence had a calming effect on her, and she needed that right now.

The doctor was a rotund bald man, who shook hands with both of them. "I'm Dr. Donovan," he said. "I've met you and your family in the hospital, Anna, but you may not remember me. Many patients don't after they've had a head injury. Sometimes it's because of their concussions and sometimes it's because of the medication we give them."

Anna squinted at the doctor and then apologized. "I'm sorry, I don't."

"That's okay, I've been told I have a forgettable face, although my wife likes it," the doctor jested. "How have you been feeling?"

"Fine," Anna answered, clasping her hands on her lap.

"*Fine* as in you don't want to complain in front of your fiancé, or *fine* as in you haven't had any nausea, fatigue, headaches or blurred vision at all? Most patients do, you know," the doctor stated, settling into a chair.

"Well, my head feels a bit heavy but I wouldn't say it aches, and I suppose my energy isn't what it usually is," she admitted. "The other day I had a pretty severe bout of nausea, too."

"Has that happened often?" the doctor asked.

"Only once." Anna dipped her head and scraped at her thumbnail. "But it was because my friend handles his buggy like a madman."

"I see. Well, that's understandable. And how about your moods, how are they?"

Anna bit her lip. "With the grace of *Gott*, I try to be *gut*-natured, but I'm afraid I don't always succeed."

"I'm sure you do your best, Anna," Dr. Donovan said and his eyes twinkled. "But what I mean is, are there times when you experience extreme mood swings? Times when you've felt exceedingly angry or despondent, or even elated? Anything like that?"

She hesitated, wondering if her ambiguous feelings about the wedding qualified as mood swings, before shaking her head.

"It's not extreme, but I have noticed Anna is weepier than she was before the accident," Fletcher offered. "She seems on the verge of tears more often than not."

"Does she—" Dr. Donovan began to ask Fletcher, but then rephrased the question and directed it toward Anna instead. "Do you suffer any prolonged periods of crying? Times when you just can't stop? Or any other unprovoked outbursts of emotion?"

"*Neh*, nothing like that," she stated.

The doctor smiled. "I suppose with four brothers at home, there's plenty to provoke an outburst now and then, isn't there?"

The three of them chuckled before Dr. Donovan continued, this time asking Fletcher, "Have you noticed any other differences in Anna's temperament?"

Fletcher replied carefully, "She's, er, less relaxed than she used to be. Not as easygoing."

Heat rose in Anna's cheeks. She realized she'd

felt tearful and tense lately, but she regretted it was so obvious to others. Was her behavior off-putting to Fletcher?

Dr. Donovan must have caught her expression because he winked at her and joshed, "When your fiancé suffers a traumatic brain injury, we'll see how relaxed he feels, right?"

"I didn't mean to sound critical," Fletcher said, and it was his turn to blush. "I only meant to point out a difference."

"It was good you did," the doctor replied. "I asked about it because it's important for me to be informed immediately if Anna experiences any extreme mood changes, like those I mentioned. That said, many head and brain injury patients are generally out of sorts following their accidents. Some of that is due to residual pain, some of it's a medication side effect and some of it is because they're quite literally not themselves. At least, not until their brains are fully recovered. It takes patience. Which may be very frustrating and even frightening for them as well as for the people who care about them. But it's all part of the healing process."

Anna leaned back in her chair, reassured by the doctor's assertion that what she was experiencing was both normal and temporary.

"How is your memory, Anna?" he asked. "Do

you recall what happened the day before the accident? How about the week before? The month?"

With each question, Anna shook her head. They discussed what she did recall—confirming her latest preaccident memories were of late August—and then the doctor performed a brief examination, looking into her eyes and checking her neurological reflexes.

"Overall, I'm pleased with your progress," he said when he completed the exam. "Your scans look good—great, in fact. I think the nausea you described will subside in time, especially now that you're not taking any medication."

"I'm glad to hear that," Anna responded politely. "But what about my memory loss?"

"You do have a longer period of amnesia than most," Dr. Donovan admitted. "It's called retrograde amnesia—meaning, you can't recall things that happened before the accident. Most people lose a few minutes, a couple of hours or even a day or two. You've lost about five or six months of memory. Now, before you get too worried, I'll tell you I've had patients who have lost up to three years!"

This fact was little consolation to her and judging from the wrinkles across Fletcher's forehead, he wasn't finding it to be reassuring, either.

"Your memories could return like that," Dr.

Donovan said and snapped his fingers. "Or, more likely, they could come over time. Sometimes, patients will experience random memories we call *islands of memory*, because they might recall certain details of an event, but not the surrounding circumstances."

Anna bent toward him, her hands folded as if in prayer. "But isn't there anything I can do to hasten my memories to return?" she asked.

Fletcher heard the note of desperation in Anna's voice and it echoed his own feelings.

"I've had patients' families and friends try to recreate lost memories for them. Others surround themselves with familiar scents. Some people insist sage tea helped their memories return. I've even known people to try hypnotism," answered Dr. Donovan. "What I recommend is getting plenty of rest."

"I've been resting all week," Anna asserted. "But I have a job. I'm a clerk at a shop in town and I think I'm ready to return to work now."

Dr. Donovan crossed his arms. "I'd highly recommend you don't. In fact, you shouldn't do any more than what you've done at home this week, both mentally and physically. It will sound funny, but you need to avoid thinking too much. I'd also advise minimal reading and problem solving. Nothing involving lengthy periods of close concentration, such as sewing. And no strenuous activities. No pitching hay, no floor scrubbing, nothing more vigorous than collecting eggs from the henhouse. I'd suggest limiting your exertion to a slow, daily stroll in the fresh air."

"But I have to help prepare the house for the wedding," Anna protested and her eyes welled.

Dr. Donovan raised his brows at Fletcher. "I'm certain your fiancé would rather have his bride healthy than anything else, right?"

Whether Anna actually became his bride or not, Fletcher agreed her health was paramount. "Anna, if rest is what it takes for you to recover and your memory to return, I'm sure Naomi will take over until you're better," he reasoned.

Dr. Donovan held up his hand. "I want to caution you both that while rest *may* be helpful in restoring Anna's memory, there's no guarantee. But the benefits of rest—for both body and mind—greatly outweigh the risks of overexertion at this point. Further, the more pressure Anna is under, the less likely she is to get the memory results you both want. So, take each day as it comes and keep your expectations in check. And remember, it's crucial that Anna doesn't experience a lot of stress or become too upset."

Fletcher and Anna both nodded without replying.

"Why such long faces?" the doctor inquired.

"Anna is recovering well, whether or not her memory returns. There's a good chance it will, but if it doesn't, it's a loss but it's not the end of the world. You have your entire lives together to make new memories, right?"

Fletcher cleared his throat and spoke deliberately. "Anna and I only met in September. She has no recollection of me and we're scheduled to be wed in about a month. We have certain... certain concerns."

Dr. Donovan blew the air out of his cheeks and took off his glasses to rub his eyes. "Ah, I understand now," he said, before readjusting his frames behind his ears. Slanting forward, he said, "I see how that could be problematic. But it also might be one of the best blessings a couple could ever receive. There's no thrill like falling in love with each other for the first time. It sounds as if you two have the opportunity to experience that joy twice!"

From the corner of his eye, Fletcher could see Anna's cheeks blossom with pink. Amish couples didn't usually speak of such intimate matters to anyone, much less to *Englisch* acquaintances, but Dr. Donovan didn't seem to notice their embarrassment.

He rolled his chair back, saying, "Alright, then, I'd like to see you back here in two weeks unless any of your symptoms worsen instead of improve. Meanwhile, have a little fun getting to know each other again. Falling in love is a gift. It's something to celebrate."

Fletcher realized the kind man meant his words to be encouraging, but as he shook the doctor's hand goodbye, he thought this felt nothing like a time of celebration. Indeed, while they journeyed back toward Willow Creek, Anna seemed somber, as well. He wasn't ready to discuss what the doctor said about her memory returning or how they might spend the next couple of weeks, so Fletcher was relieved when she didn't broach those topics, either. But she remained quiet for so long he finally asked if the journey was nauseating her.

"*Neh*, not at all. This has been a very smooth ride," she replied. "I was just thinking how disappointed Joseph will be to learn I can't yet return to the shop."

"Are *you* disappointed?" Fletcher asked.

Anna giggled. "To be honest, *neh*, not really. I'd much rather help Naomi manage the household. And I'll admit that it's been necessary for me to rest in between tasks recently, which I couldn't do at the shop. I worry I wouldn't be efficient there, even if I were allowed to return. But I feel bad leaving Joseph shorthanded. The store was packed with customers when I stopped by the other morning."

Fletcher pulled on the rein and the horse turned toward the right, exiting the main roadway. "Would it be possible for Melinda to temporarily take your place?"

"Jah!" Anna practically hopped up from the seat. "What a great idea, Fletcher! I'm sure she'll prefer working in town, and I dare say Naomi will appreciate having her out of her hair for a while."

Fletcher grinned, pleased he could provide Anna with a satisfactory solution to at least one of the problems she was facing. Her praise always made his chest swell and today, it gave him hope that they might be able to work out whatever other concerns she had, too. But first, he'd have to help her remember them, of course. So, before dropping her off for the evening, he said, "I'll have to work late tomorrow and Friday night because I left early today, but I'd like to take you out alone on Saturday, if I may?"

"Denki, I'd like that." Her cheek dimpled as she replied.

Fletcher felt so encouraged that when he returned home, he took out his toolbox for the first time since receiving Anna's note and began working on his wedding gift for her: he was re-sectioning one area of the parlor into an alcove so she could have privacy for reading and writing in her journal. As he was sanding a length of board, he began thinking about ways in which he could help jog Anna's memory without pressuring her. By the time he put away his tools for the night, he was so eager for the date he'd planned that he almost hoped her memory wouldn't come back before he had a chance to see her again.

Chapter Four

Upon waking on Saturday morning, Anna kept her eyes closed, hoping her memory had been restored overnight. Once again, she was disappointed that nothing from the past six months came to mind. She blinked to see Melinda rummaging through a drawer. Usually Anna was awake long before her cousin, who required considerable rousing to get out of bed, especially after she'd been out with Aaron the previous night. Anna figured Melinda must be excited about beginning her first day of work at Schrock's Shop.

"Guder mariye," Melinda sang out. "Do you suppose I might borrow a few hair clips?"

Anna yawned as she pushed herself onto her elbows. "I gave you my hair clips earlier in the week. Did you misplace them?"

"Neh, you never gave them to me," Melinda

replied. "Perhaps you gave some to Naomi, but not to me."

"I'm certain I gave them to you," Anna insisted. "In fact, I was running low myself but I let you use them because it hurt my head to gather my hair tightly. Don't you remember?"

Melinda shrugged. "*Neh*, but that's okay. Naomi probably has extras."

Anna didn't mind about the hair clips in particular as much as she minded the fact Melinda denied Anna gave her the accessories in the first place. How could Melinda be that inattentive? Before Anna could think of a kind way to point out her carelessness, the young woman hurried from the room.

Anna dressed quickly and scurried into the kitchen, too. Fletcher had already picked up Roy and Raymond for their half day of work, and he'd bring them home at dinnertime, too, since he was taking Anna on an outing. Meanwhile, she decided to offer to transport Melinda into town. Whether unintentionally or not, the doctor hadn't expressly prohibited Anna from handling the horse and buggy, and she was feeling cooped up. Besides, she wanted to purchase more hairpins so she could tidy her appearance before going out with Fletcher.

When Anna suggested to Naomi that she wanted to take Melinda to Schrock's, her stepmother replied, "*Denki*, but I have to go to town anyway to buy baking supplies."

"Why don't you let me pick them up?" Anna asked, knowing the heavy Saturday traffic would be unsettling to Naomi, who was easily flustered by the *Englisch* trucks and tour buses.

"*Neh*, I need to buy in bulk, in preparation for our wedding guests," she countered. "The items will be too heavy for you to carry. The doctor's list prohibits heavy lifting, remember?"

"I'll take Eli and Evan with me. They're strong—they can carry the packages. If they're especially helpful, we might even stop at Yoder's Bakery for a treat afterward," Anna bargained. "I'll be fine."

"*Jah*, we'll help Anna. Please can we go, *Mamm*?" pleaded Evan.

"It will keep us out from underfoot," Eli reasoned, using one of his *mamm*'s expressions for effect, "instead of muddying your freshly scrubbed floors."

"*Jah*, alright, but you'll still have to complete your chores when you return," Naomi warned the boys as they shot out the door ahead of Anna and Melinda.

On the way, as Eli and Evan were distracted in the back seat with dividing the shopping list between them, Anna again brought up the topic of the hair clips. "I can replace the pins, Melinda," she said. "But it troubled me to hear you say I never gave them to you. You need to be more focused. If a customer at Schrock's gives you a large bill and you aren't paying attention, you may neglect to give them their correct change. That will create problems for everyone."

"I'm quite certain that won't happen," Melinda said breezily. "After all, I'm not the one with amnesia."

Anna's ears were ringing, but she responded calmly. "What do you mean by that?"

"Only that I don't recall you ever giving me your hairpins, so I have to believe you're mistaken. It's not your fault, necessarily. You're probably just remembering it wrong."

Anna squeezed her eyes shut and inhaled through her nose and then blew the air out through her mouth. She opened her eyes and moderated her voice to state, "Melinda, I gave you the hairpins after my accident and after I ceased taking any medication. I remember everything from the past week perfectly."

Melinda wrinkled her nose. "Why are you getting so prickly about such a trivial matter?" But before Anna responded, Melinda shrieked, "Oh, take the reins, will you? I can jump out at this stop sign instead of walking to Schrock's from the horse and buggy lot. See you later!"

As Melinda bounced down from the buggy

and tore through traffic, Eli exclaimed, "Everyone knows you're not supposed to do that! Doesn't she have any common sense?"

Shaking her head, Anna wondered the same thing herself. In the pause it took for traffic to start moving again, Melinda scudded across the street and pulled open the door to Schrock's. Watching her, Anna feared her cousin might not even last a week in the shop before Joseph would have to let her go. He'd be short staffed again and Anna would feel obligated to return, since she was the one who recommended Melinda for the temporary position. *In that case, I better make hay while the sun shines*, she thought. *Or at least make my dress while I have a chance.* Although the doctor had prohibited prolonged periods of sewing, Anna figured she could stitch it together a bit at a time, but first she'd need to purchase her wedding dress fabric.

After all of the groceries had been secured in the buggy, Anna shepherded the boys into Yoder's Bakery, where she treated them to a cup of cocoa each and allowed them to split one of Faith Yoder's renowned apple fry pies.

"How are you?" Faith asked with a look of concern. "We heard you took a bad fall."

"*Denki*, I feel fine now." Anna deliberately kept her answer vague; she didn't want to lie, nor did she wish to tell anyone else about her memory problems, lest they question her about her wedding plans, as well. "How about you? Is your business thriving in its new location?"

"*Jah*. It's made such a difference to have a shop on Main Street instead of working out of the kitchen at home," Faith said. "I'm already up to my eyeballs in Easter orders for my *Englisch* customers' celebrations. Oh! That reminds me, are you planning to order a wedding cake?"

Although many of the desserts at Amish weddings were homemade by the bride's family and friends, it was common for the bride to order at least one special-made cake from a professional baker, as well, and Anna didn't know quite how to reply. She figured it was one thing to buy fabric for a wedding dress at this point, but it was entirely another to order a wedding cake.

Despite experiencing the first sweet stirrings of infatuation for Fletcher, Anna realized that if her memory didn't return in full, there was still the possibility they wouldn't marry. If the wedding was called off, she could always wear her dress to church, since it would be in the same pattern as the rest of her clothes. But if she placed an order for a cake, Faith might turn down future business so that she would have time to fill Anna's order. Anna didn't want to inconvenience Faith and affect her business like that.

"Er," she hedged. "I'm not quite certain."

Faith's creamy complexion splotched with pink. "Of course, that's fine. I only asked because your wedding date is so close to Easter, I wanted to be sure to reserve time to make your cake if you wanted one. I wasn't trying to pressure you into ordering anything from me—"

"*Neh*, I didn't think you were." Anna stammered, "It's just that I... I haven't made up my mind yet."

"Better you should wait, then." Faith chuckled. "Your cousin Melinda ordered hers last week and she's already changed her mind three times. I'm not going to stock up on any specialty ingredients for hers until the week before the wedding, when I give her a final deadline."

"*Gut* idea." Anna laughed. "I'll be sure to place my order as soon as I've given it more thought. Meanwhile, would you mind if I leave Eli and Evan here to finish their cocoa? I need to make a last-minute purchase from the mercantile. They'll behave themselves, won't you, boys?"

"With six brothers, I know how to keep these two out of mischief," Faith jested.

Anna was glad for the opportunity to shop for the fabric without the boys around. The two of them had eyes and ears for everything, and she was concerned they might report her purchase back to Naomi, who would fret endlessly about Anna sewing, no matter how many breaks she took. Anna swiftly backtracked down Main Street to the mercantile, but selecting the color took more time than she'd anticipated. Brides in her district tended to choose a traditional blue for their wedding dresses, although some, like Melinda, favored brighter variations, such as shades of purple. Anna liked both colors, but neither particularly appealed to her over the other.

She was fingering a swatch of navy blue cotton when she caught sight of a bolt in a deep green hue. It reminded her of the shade of the grass beneath a willow tree. She'd be pleased to have a new dress in that color, regardless of whether it ended up being her wedding dress or not. And somehow, just the act of selecting the fabric made her feel more confident about the future. She bought enough for herself and her two *newehockers* and hustled back to the bakery, knowing Naomi would begin to worry if she and the boys didn't return home soon. A young Amish woman was exiting Yoder's with a stack of cardboard boxes full of treats in her arms and two bags of doughnuts swinging from her hand as Anna was entering.

"Excuse me," Anna apologized, peering around the large package of fabric she carried.

The woman held the door open for her with her elbow as she balanced her own packages.

"*Denki*, but I don't think there's room for me to squeeze by. I'm just here to summon my brothers anyway." Anna smiled, calling, "Eli, Evan, *kumme* please."

The woman made a discontented huffing noise as the boys passed her.

When they were out of earshot, Anna instructed, "Boys, it's only proper to hold the door for someone who has packages in her hands, even when she's being very polite and holding it for you. I think you offended that lady."

"I'm sorry, Anna. We'll remember that next time," Evan promised.

"*Jah*," agreed Eli. "I didn't want to get my handprints on the door handle. But we'll apologize to Katie Fisher at church on Sunday."

"That was my friend Katie Fisher, Tessa's sister?" Anna asked abashedly.

Suddenly she understood why Katie had acted so crabby: it must have seemed as if Anna was snubbing her, just as she'd apparently snubbed her sister, Tessa. Anna pressed her lips together, silently praying for her memory to return before she hurt anyone else's feelings or had to tell another person about her amnesia.

Fletcher pried the lid off a paint can. Painting was no one's favorite part of the job, but it was a necessary one. He wanted to be certain Raymond and Roy took as much care performing the mundane aspects of their responsibilities as they did the more challenging tasks.

"We'll have to move up our completion date on this site," Aaron announced. "I accepted another project that begins next week."

Fletcher voiced his surprise. "This office suite is going to require hanging more than the usual amount of trim, which we don't even have on hand yet."

"*Jah*, that's why I'm heading to the lumber store now."

"Now?" Fletcher repeated. If Aaron left, they'd fall behind on the painting.

"It's not as if I can call them on my cell phone, is it?" Aaron cracked. "If I don't talk to them today, I won't know if they have what we need in stock."

Fletcher hesitated. "The boys and I could stop on our way to their house after work today," he suggested.

"*Neh*, I'll go now," Aaron insisted.

To Fletcher, it seemed a waste of time and manpower for Aaron to run errands during the workday when Fletcher offered to do it off the clock, but he knew that was Aaron's decision to make, not his, since Aaron was the foreman. After giving it more thought, Fletcher concluded he'd prefer to arrive at Anna's sooner rather than later anyway, so he could finally spend an afternoon alone with her, helping her to recall the past. As he painted he silently asked God to bless their time together, and before Fletcher knew it, Roy signaled that it was nearly dinnertime.

At Anna's house, Evan and Eli zipped pell-mell across the yard to greet them.

"Fletcher!" Eli shouted. "*Mamm* says you're joining us for dinner. We made certain to taste test your food for mushrooms—just like Nehemiah did for King Artaxerxes in the Bible."

"Really?" asked Fletcher. "I didn't realize King Artaxerxes was allergic to mushrooms, too."

"Not mushrooms but anything poisonous," Eli explained solemnly.

Fletcher nodded seriously and clapped Eli's shoulder in return. "I appreciate that."

When Fletcher entered the kitchen, Naomi was slicing bread. Anna had just slid a pan from the oven and her cheeks were glowing. She gave him a little half wave with the oversize oven mitts she wore on her hands and then giggled at herself. He hadn't realized how much he'd missed her spontaneous sense of humor and he suddenly felt unnerved by her charm.

"Hello, Naomi. Hello, Anna," he said. "You smell *appenditlich*."

He'd meant to say the *food* smelled delicious,

but before he could correct his mistake, Evan hooted, "Fletcher said, 'you smell *appenditlich*' instead of 'the food smells *appenditlich*'!"

"Beheef dich," Anna shushed Evan with the command to behave himself before giving him a playful swat with the oven mitt. "Go wash your hands, please."

"I'd better wash my hands, too." Fletcher quickly ducked into the washroom until his ears lost their crimson flush.

After the meal, he informed Anna she might want to wear a heavier shawl, as they'd be spending time near the creek, where the air was especially cool.

"You're going to the creek?" Eli asked. "Can we *kumme*, too? We finished all of our chores."

"Jah. We can look for Timothy again," Evan begged. "Please?"

For a split second, Fletcher feared Anna would allow Eli and Evan to accompany them, but then she glanced in Fletcher's direction and gave him a wink.

"I think the turtles are still in brumation," she said. "Besides, you boys already went on an outing with me today. Now it's Fletcher's turn."

Satisfied, Fletcher uncrossed his arms, but there was still a delay before he set out with Anna: she insisted on washing and drying the dishes, despite Naomi's protests. When they were finally seated in the buggy and traveling down the lane, he glanced sideways to see Anna smiling broadly.

"Look!" she exclaimed, pointing to a robin in the field. "I guess that means winter is officially over, although our winter was so mild this year, it was as if it hardly happened."

"You remembered our mild winter?" Fletcher asked, unable to keep the tension from his voice.

"*Neh*, Naomi told me," Anna confessed. "I'm sorry if I got your hopes up. I assure you, as soon I remember anything from the past six months, I'll let you know."

"Of course you will." Fletcher hadn't meant to sound as if he were pressuring her. He loosened his grip on the reins and lightened his tone. "We did have a white *Grischtdaag*, though. The landscape was blanketed in pristine perfection."

"So then, white must be your favorite color?" Anna asked him cheekily. "And winter must be your favorite season?"

"*Neh*, spring is my favorite season—same as yours. And green is my favorite color," he answered, thinking in particular of the green radiance of Anna's eyes.

"Oh, that's interesting to know," Anna replied. "Because today I purchased green fabric for my wedding dress."

Fletcher again felt a surge of apprehension.

She was making her dress, which was another significant step in the wedding preparations. Although that was a good sign, he had to remind himself that once Anna's memories returned, it was possible she'd cancel the wedding to him in favor of a renewed courtship with Aaron. Even so, Fletcher allowed himself a small measure of optimism.

They rode in silence until they came to the public park that hosted the stony path running adjacent to the creek. Following the trail, they eventually arrived at the same spot Anna and her brothers frequented by cutting down the hill and through the meadow directly behind their house.

"We could have walked straight to the creek from my house," Anna noted. "I'm not as fragile as everyone seems to think I am."

"*Jah*, but the creek isn't the only stop on our itinerary," Fletcher replied as he pulled a blanket and thermos from the back of his buggy. "We'll need the buggy to travel to the other place we'll visit today."

"As long as our next destination isn't Tessa and Katie Fisher's house," she remarked. "I'm afraid I've managed to slight them both on separate occasions. I had no idea who they were and I feel awful I don't remember them." Anna sighed.

"You'll remember them yet," Fletcher encouraged her.

When they reached the water's edge, Fletcher spread the blanket he'd been carrying beneath a barely budding willow tree and motioned for Anna to have a seat. Then he poured fragrant hot liquid from the thermos into a cup and presented it to her.

"What's this?" she questioned.

"It's sage tea," he replied, filling a cup for himself. "Remember? Dr. Donovan said he had patients who claimed it helped their memories return."

Anna pursed her lips to blow on the steaming drink. "He also said some of his patients practiced hypnotism. You're not going to try to hypnotize me, too, are you?"

Fletcher could tell by the way her cheek dimpled that she was pleased rather than annoyed. "*Neh*. But he did say it was important to get rest—which is why we're going to relax here for a while."

"Oh, I see," Anna said with a lilt in her voice. "We're not merely whiling away a Saturday afternoon. We're actually following doctor's orders?"

"Doctor's orders," Fletcher reiterated, enjoying their flirtation. "Actually, we're following his orders and his patients' suggestions. He mentioned some of their families and friends tried to recreate memories in order to jog the patients' recollection. There's no pressure, but I hope these surroundings might prompt memories of our early days together. You see, I hadn't been in town for more than a week when I first met you fishing down at the bend in the creek."

"I was fishing?" Anna was surprised. "But I've never liked handling grubs."

Fletcher gave a hearty laugh, exposing nearly perfectly aligned teeth, except for one at the top left corner, which was slightly crooked, as if it didn't quite fit among the others.

"Neh," he said. "I meant *I* was fishing. You were leaning against a willow on the embankment."

"Just loitering there?" That didn't sound like something she would have done, either.

"Actually, you were weeping," Fletcher admitted.

Anna's cheeks went hot when she heard Fletcher had first encountered her in such a vulnerable state. "I'm afraid I did a lot of crying in the months following my *daed*'s death."

"Perhaps, but when I made a dumb joke about suddenly understanding why the tree was called a *weeping* willow, you were gracious enough to laugh."

"You don't expect me to start weeping under this willow again now, do you?" Anna bantered.

"Neh," Fletcher replied. "If there's one thing I hate, it's seeing you in tears."

Fletcher's response was so earnest it warmed Anna to the tips of her toes. She looked around and noted, "I've always appreciated what a peaceful place this is."

Fletcher guffawed. "That's the very thing we first argued about."

"We did?" Anna's curiosity was piqued. "Why?"

"Well, after I met you here the first time and you were crying—you hadn't yet confided the reasons behind your tears—I made that dumb joke, but then I contrived an excuse to leave, so you'd have your privacy."

"That was kind of you," Anna commented.

"Not really," Fletcher admitted. "I was agitated because I believed our voices had scared away the fish. See, I'd specifically chosen this spot instead of the location upstream where everyone else was fishing because it seemed more peaceful here. So, when you showed up the next evening, we got into a bit of an argument about who had more of a right to be here."

"You were a newcomer to our community," Anna said. "I'm sorry I wasn't friendlier. That was rude of me."

"Neh, what's rude is what I did on the third evening."

Listening to Fletcher talk about their first

encounter was like reading a very good book: Anna wanted to hear all of it at once yet she didn't want the story to come to an end.

"What did you do on the third evening?" she asked.

"I presented you with a pen and a journal and suggested you might benefit from writing about your heartache instead of reflecting on it here at the stream," Fletcher said, cringing at himself. "What a heel."

"You weren't a heel. I can be a bit territorial— my *daed* always said it came from living as an only child for so long and not having to share my space. I was being selfish."

"*Neh,*" Fletcher countered. "*What a heel* is what you wrote about me on the first page of the diary I'd given you. You scribbled, *This journal was given to me by Fletcher Chupp, what a heel.* And then you thrust the diary under my nose to show me what it said."

"I did?" Anna was mortified. "That was childish."

"It was *true*. I was being a heel. I cared more about fishing than about your feelings. And I tried to disguise my self-centeredness with a gift."

"How did we ever end up courting after introductions like ours?" she asked.

"It's simple—we got to know each other. I

kept coming here to fish and you kept coming here to be alone with your thoughts. Neither of us had the privacy we needed to accomplish our purpose, but we were both too stubborn to budge, so we began talking to each other instead. Soon, there was nothing we didn't tell each other. Nothing," Fletcher said.

When he looked at her, his eyes were dark as the midnight sky and his voice was husky with ardor. A subtle yet familiar emotion stirred inside of Anna and she shivered.

"What is it?" Fletcher asked, sitting up straight. "Did you remember something just then?"

"Almost," she said, sorry to disappoint him. "But it was more of a feeling than a memory."

"A happy feeling?"

"Decidedly so." She smiled, holding his gaze.

"Gut." He stood and took her empty cup. "There's another important stop along our stroll down memory lane, so we ought to get going now."

As they were returning to the buggy, Anna suddenly uttered, "The journal you gave me! Surely I must have recorded my memories in there."

"I hadn't even thought of that, but you're right," Fletcher agreed. "When was the last time you wrote in it?"

"Wrote in it? I didn't even know it existed! Where do I keep it?"

"I don't know. You told me you wrote in it all the time but you had to squirrel it away in a secret place because you didn't want the boys happening upon it."

"Really?" Anna was deflated. "Well, what did it look like?"

"It was about this big," Fletcher answered, squaring his hands, "and it had a brown leather jacket with a little gold lock attached at the side."

"I'll search for it as soon as I get home," Anna said enthusiastically as Fletcher supported her into the buggy. "It must hold a storehouse of memories."

Fletcher's palms grew sweaty as he contemplated what Anna might find written in her journal. He'd gotten so caught up in the nostalgia of first meeting her that he'd momentarily lost sight of the fact his ultimate intention for the outing was to help her recall her hesitation about marrying him, so he could address it. He removed his hat and swept his hand through his hair, as if to brush away the troublesome thoughts.

"Someone's been painting today, I see," Anna noticed. "You've got flecks of white in your hair."

"If you think my hair is bad, you ought to see

Roy's and Raymond's," he replied. "Their saving grace is that they're blond, rather than dark like me, so it doesn't show up as much."

"*Denki* for mentoring them, Fletcher. I don't know what Naomi would do without a man around to train them in a vocation."

"It's a privilege," Fletcher said soberly. "Now, as you know, to the right is Turner King's *daadi haus*, but we won't drop in there until you resolve your misunderstanding with Katie and Tessa. A little farther along the lane is our house."

Anna hesitated when Fletcher turned in the driveway. "I'm not sure it's appropriate for the two of us to spend time together unchaperoned here. I wouldn't want people to see us and think—"

"Of course not. Neither would I," Fletcher said. He shared Anna's commitment to modesty and decorum. "I only want to show you something. Wait here and I'll be right out with it."

He scooted into the house and emerged carrying a black suit on a hanger.

"I don't suppose you recall making this?" he asked.

"Hmm, I don't know." Anna scrunched her brows together and teased, "That stitching doesn't look like mine. Are you sure *you* didn't make the suit?"

"These hands can work a hammer, but not a sewing needle," Fletcher argued.

"*Jah*, that would explain why the side seam appears crooked."

"It's not crooked, you're looking at it askance."

Anna giggled. "One thing is certain—you will look very dapper in that, indeed. Now please go put it away. I'm freezing," she said.

Despite his best efforts to guard his emotions, Fletcher felt his knees go weak and his hopes grow strong because of Anna's compliment. He whistled as he brought the suit inside and quickly returned to take Anna home. He idled at the end of the lane as another buggy sailed past. Even if he hadn't recognized the familiar style of the carriage, he knew only one person who worked his horse that hard.

"That was Aaron," Anna said, as if reading his thoughts. "He probably picked Melinda up after her first day at the shop. Look at him go! I'm queasy just watching him."

Anna's remark cast doubt on Fletcher's concern about her affection for Aaron, and he chuckled zealously. As they rode, she peppered him with questions about his work as a carpenter, his sisters and their families, his likes and dislikes, and other important aspects of his life.

Finally, he teased, "There isn't going to be a quiz about this, Anna."

"*Neh*, but I want to learn as much about you as I can as quickly as I can, Fletcher Chupp."

Fletcher drew the horse to an abrupt halt and shifted to study her face in the waning light. "Why did you say that?" he asked, his voice throaty.

She tipped her head. "I said it because I meant it."

"That's exactly what you said—and I do mean word for word—when I first began walking out with you," he explained. "I thought maybe you'd remembered saying it."

"*Neh*, but it's still true," she responded. "Rather, it's true again."

As he clicked to the horse, Fletcher's stomach turned somersaults. Dr. Donovan was right: there was nothing more exhilarating than falling in love, and he was on the brink of falling for Anna a second time.

"Whoa, steady," he commanded the horse, directing it down the lane to Anna's house. He might as well have been talking to his own heart, which seemed in danger of rearing wildly and galloping away with him. He couldn't allow himself to forget Anna's note, even if she had.

"Look, Aaron has hitched his horse," Anna pointed out. "That must mean he's staying for supper. You're *wilkom* to join us, too."

"*Denki*, but I have work to do at home,"

Fletcher said. He needed to clear his head. Besides, he didn't want to take advantage of Naomi's hospitality, even if his cousin was staying, so he walked Anna to the porch, but before he could say goodbye, the door swung open. The tantalizing aroma of pork chops filled Fletcher's nostrils and when Naomi insisted he stay for supper, he couldn't refuse. This time when everyone joined hands for grace, Anna gave his palm a quick squeeze before letting go, and when he accidentally knocked his knee into hers, she didn't flinch or move her chair.

"How was your first day at the shop?" Anna asked Melinda as they were eating dessert.

"Easy as pie," Melinda replied. "No wonder you prefer working there to helping us at home."

"Anna's reputation for industriousness is what afforded you a temporary position at Schrock's Shop," Naomi diplomatically reminded her niece. "But because you've had such an easy day there, Melinda, you may clear the table and wash and dry the dishes, as well. I'm sure Aaron has chores to get to at home and will be leaving straightaway, too. As it is, I've got mending to do and the boys need to take a bath. *Kumme*, Evan and Eli, say *gut nacht* to everyone. Roy and Raymond, the wood bin is running low."

"I'll walk outside with you," Fletcher suggested to Aaron after Naomi and the boys left the room, fearing his cousin wouldn't take the hint that it was time to leave.

"Okay," he agreed amiably. "But first I have something to give Anna. It's in my buggy."

Anna stopped rinsing the pan in her hands long enough to shrug her shoulders and cast a puzzled look at Melinda. Fletcher stood by the door of the mudroom until Aaron returned with a pot of pale blue flowers.

"For you," he said, extending it to Anna.

She looked confused. *"Denki,"* she said, accepting the pot. "How thoughtful."

Melinda clapped her hands and tittered. "They're forget-me-nots, get it? You know, because you have amnesia. I was telling Aaron about the hair clips as we drove by the nursery in town and he was suddenly inspired. He said the flowers would make the perfect get-well gift for you!"

"I get it. *Denki,*" Anna repeated, red-faced, before abruptly saying good-night to everyone and excusing herself from the room.

Fletcher strode to his buggy without waiting for Aaron to stop laughing with Melinda. Filling his lungs with the night air, he tried not to rush to conclusions about the name of the flower Aaron had chosen for Anna. He was familiar enough with Aaron's sense of humor to know that his cousin's jokes were often misplaced. It was entirely possible there was no hidden message—other than the obvious pun in reference to amnesia—intended by his choice of flowers. As for Anna leaving the room so quickly, perhaps she merely felt nauseated or tired.

Yet as the horse pulled his buggy toward home, Fletcher noticed the optimism he'd felt earlier in the day was replaced by a gnawing insecurity that he couldn't seem to shake. *Dear Lord*, he began to pray, but then he stopped. Unsure of what to ask for, he kept his request simple: *please help*.

Chapter Five

After retreating to the washroom to splash water on her face, Anna patted her cheeks dry with a towel. Over the course of her relationship with Aaron, she'd grown accustomed to overlooking his jokes and pranks, and once again she reminded herself that his intention was to make her laugh, not to mock her condition. Recalling that Dr. Donovan said it was normal for head injury patients to be hypersensitive during their recoveries, she decided rather than to waste any more time feeling irritated, she'd turn her attention to searching her bedroom for the journal Fletcher had given her.

When she didn't find it, she searched again a second time, patting beneath her mattress, opening every drawer and examining the shelf in her closet. Like most Amish homes, theirs was furnished simply and contained little clutter, so finding lost items was usually only a matter of retracing one's steps. Unfortunately, Anna's amnesia kept her from being able to do that.

She shone the flashlight into the other half of the attic, which was completely empty except for the package containing the wedding dress fabric she'd stashed there that afternoon because she was afraid Naomi might reproach her for sewing if she happened upon it in Anna's closet. Although Anna knew it would be unlikely for her to keep a personal item like a journal elsewhere in the house, she checked each room and asked each family member if they might have known where she'd put it.

"You're always writing in it, so you'd better find it soon," Melinda answered as she furiously scoured a pan. "It would be a shame if someone discovered your secrets."

To Anna's ears, that almost sounded like a taunt. Did Melinda know something she wasn't saying about the journal? Had she read it? Almost immediately, Anna was filled with shame. Assuming ill of another person was not the Amish way. Besides, Fletcher said the diary had a lock, so when Anna found the key on a string inside her drawer, she immediately looped it around her neck.

"I'm not concerned about someone discovering my secrets," she replied affably, picking up a towel to dry the dishes stacking up next to the sink. "But the diary could go a long way in helping me regain my memory, so please keep your eye out for it. Now, how about if you tell me more about your first day at the shop?"

Melinda was pleased to regale Anna with descriptions of the *Englischers* who came into the shop, recounting their questions and comments, and detailing their purchases. Listening to Melinda's exuberance about the experience, Anna was glad her cousin had the opportunity to work outside their home. Perhaps by representing the Amish community's wares to *Englisch* customers, Melinda might take better care to reflect Amish values, too.

By the time they finished cleaning the dishes, any tension Anna experienced concerning Aaron's gift had been washed away, as well. But her head felt as heavy as an anvil and she retired to her bedroom early. She searched her drawers and under the bed one last time, wishing she could find her journal. Not only did she want to read what she'd already written there, but she wanted to record her current feelings about Fletcher, in order to make sense of them. She found him to be thoughtful, respectful and fun, as well as strong, handsome and Godly. It was no wonder she'd been smitten with him from the start.

Yet, as she leaned against her bed to unlace

her shoes, she ruminated that being infatuated wasn't reason enough to marry someone. She didn't doubt she professed to the deacon after their meetings concluded that she believed Fletcher was the husband the Lord provided for her. But despite her growing affection for Fletcher, Anna just didn't know if she could honestly make that same vow again when the bishop asked her to affirm it during the wedding ceremony in church.

Anna slipped into a kneeling position on the floor and folded her hands, beseeching, *Please, Lord, return my memory to me soon. And if it's Your will, help me find my diary, as well.*

"Oh, *gut*, you're still up," Melinda said when she burst through the door. "Do you want to see the material for my wedding dress? It arrived at the mercantile today and I picked it up after work."

"Sure." Anna straightened into a standing position.

Melinda unwrapped a layer of brown paper from a large package.

"It's beautiful," Anna gushed about the violet fabric, fingering it along the edge. "This will look lovely with your brunette hair and big brown eyes."

"That's what Aaron said, too," Melinda commented as she secured the string around the bundle again.

As they donned their nightclothes, Anna realized perhaps Melinda simply didn't realize how she came across when she repeated Aaron's remarks, whether kind or far-fetched. She extinguished the lamp.

"Melinda?" Anna asked into the darkness. "Remember how you were talking about secrets and wishing I'd confide in you more often? I have a secret I'd like to share with you."

Anna could hear Melinda scramble into an attentive position. "What is it?"

"I bought my wedding dress material today, too. It's forest green. I'm not supposed to concentrate on sewing for long periods of time, but I figure I can work on it now and again, provided Naomi doesn't catch me and start to fret."

"I promise not to tell," Melinda said and flopped back down against her pillow, sighing. "I don't know where I'm going to find time to make mine now that I'm working at the shop."

"I'll tell you what," Anna offered. "The light in our room isn't the best, but perhaps we can spend a few evenings a week sewing up here together. And I'm happy to help sew yours if you find it becomes unmanageable while you're working at the shop."

"*Denki*, Anna." Melinda yawned. "I'd really appreciate that."

After a few minutes of silence, Anna was on the brink of sleep when Melinda mumbled, "I'm so happy you decided to buy your material even though you can't remember your groom. Aaron told me today that he didn't think Fletcher could handle another fiancée calling off the wedding. The first time nearly crushed him."

"What?" Anna whispered. When there was no reply, she asked again, "What did you just say?" but Melinda's breathing rose and fell in the steady pattern of sleep.

Anna listened to it all throughout the night as she tried to drum up a satisfactory reason for why Fletcher neglected to mention his previous fiancée. Instead, she just came up with additional questions, each one more alarming than the last: Why did Fletcher's first fiancée call their wedding off? If Anna had known the reason, would she still have agreed to marry him so quickly? Was there anything else he was keeping from her? If so, how would she know?

She was relieved when daylight filled the windows and she could rise and ready herself for church. The family squeezed into the buggy, three seated in the front and three seated in the back, with Evan balanced against Naomi's knees. This Sunday, they traveled to James and Amelia

Hooley's home on the other end of town. Their basement was used as the gathering room for the worship service; afterward, the men flipped the benches, fashioning them into makeshift tables for lunch. Anna was eager to speak to the Fisher sisters and she figured she'd find them in the kitchen, helping serve and clean up.

"Look who's here!" Tessa exclaimed, nudging her sister.

"I'm Ka-tie," her other friend greeted her, pronouncing her name very slowly.

"And *I'm* sorry," Anna apologized. "I'm afraid you both must think me terribly rude—"

"It. Is. Okay," Katie enunciated loudly. "Why. Don't. You. Sit. Down?"

Anna didn't know what to make of Katie's manner of speaking. Did she always talk like that? She squinted at her.

Tessa explained in equally deliberate speech. "Please don't cry. We aren't angry with you. We know about your brain injury."

"Is that why you're talking like that?" Anna inquired, suddenly realizing their strange intonations were supposed to be for her benefit. "*Jah*, I had a traumatic brain injury, which is another name for a concussion, and I'm experiencing something called retrograde amnesia, but there's nothing wrong with my hearing, I'm not about to cry and I don't need to sit down."

Tessa threw her hands in the air. "Ach! Melinda told everyone at the shop your faculties haven't been the same since your fall. Oh dear, Anna, now *we're* the ones who are sorry!"

Katie covered her face with the dishtowel. "I'm so embarrassed I could cry!"

Anna should have known Melinda was at the heart of the misunderstanding—she was such a *bobblemoul*, as Evan would say! Nevertheless, she sympathized with her friends. "That's exactly how I felt when I learned I'd accidentally slighted each of you."

"It wasn't like you at all," admitted Tessa. "I couldn't understand why you were standing me up—we'd made a date to walk over to the mercantile during my break to look at material. I thought perhaps you'd changed your mind about asking me to be a *newehocker.*"

"*Jah*, and when you made a remark about not being able to get past me at the door of the bakery, I took it as a judgment on my weight," Katie confessed. "Especially since I was carrying a load of goodies. Which, by the way, I was purchasing to bring here for dessert—it was my turn but I'd had a cold and I didn't want to spread germs by baking for everyone."

"*Neh*, not at all!" Anna assured them. "I simply couldn't—I *can't* remember any part of my life after August. The doctor says those memories may return soon and I hope they do because by all counts, I've heard we've had many *gut* times together."

"We still can," Katie suggested. "And nothing makes for a *gut* time like a treat from Faith Yoder's bakery. Follow me and I'll show you where I'm keeping a secret stash!"

Fletcher scanned the yard for Anna, wondering if she'd stepped outside for a breath of air. They had a long-standing practice of "bumping into each other" under the tallest tree in the church hosts' yards after he helped put the benches into the bench wagon and she participated in dish cleanup. He wondered if there was any chance she'd remember and meet him there that day. But beneath the Hooleys' oak, he happened upon his uncle instead of Anna.

"My knee acts up when I sit that long so I have to get out and move around," Isaiah explained to his nephew. "Especially when the weather is damp and dreary like it is today."

"It must run in the family," Fletcher replied. "My *daed* suffered from arthritis, too."

"*Jah*, I remember. Speaking of suffering, how is Anna?"

"She's not in much physical pain anymore, but her memory still hasn't returned."

"It will, son." His uncle's confidence was

comforting. Isaiah continued, "She's young. It's not like when you get to be my age. The memory just goes. The other day I climbed down a ladder to get a tool and couldn't remember what I was looking for. I climbed back up, remembered, climbed back down and forgot again by the time I reached the landing."

"No wonder your knee hurts, with all that ladder climbing." Fletcher chuckled. Then he confided, "I wish it were just a single item Anna couldn't remember. But she doesn't remember events, she doesn't remember people… She doesn't remember me."

"*Mamm* sent me to round you up, *Daed*," Aaron interrupted, suddenly present at Fletcher's side. "One of the girls has a headache and needs to get home."

"*Jah*, alright. But speaking of headaches, if you need to take Anna to her doctor appointments, you go right ahead, Fletcher, you hear?" Isaiah ordered.

"I'm glad you mentioned that, because she has a follow-up appointment on Tuesday afternoon in Highland Springs. It's possible Naomi or Ray—"

"*Neh*, it's better if you're the one who brings Anna to Highland Springs," Isaiah interjected. "I trust you to manage your workload. As for Anna not remembering you, she will. Just wait a little longer, pray a little harder and keep spending every spare moment you can with her. Either way, the more she's with you, the more she'll know you. And as they say, to know you is to love you."

"*Denki, Onkel*, that's *gut* advice," Fletcher said as Isaiah clapped him on his shoulder before meandering away. He was heartened by his uncle's perspective.

"Like *Daed* said, it's okay if you leave early Tuesday afternoon, but you'll need to clear it with me in the future if you change your schedule," Aaron remarked. "You can't just leave the site without notifying anyone where you're going or when you'll be back."

"Of course," Fletcher agreed, even though he was thinking that Aaron was the one who left the work site without telling anyone where he was going. Upon waking that morning, Fletcher had asked the Lord to forgive him for his annoyance about Aaron's get-well gift, so he didn't want to slip back into a resentful attitude. He also prayed that while he waited for Anna's memory to return, he'd be able to maintain a more positive outlook about their future. "Have you seen Anna around?"

"She and the Fisher sisters were eating doughnuts on the side porch a few minutes ago."

Approaching the house, Fletcher heard the

trio's laughter before he saw them. "That's the sound of old friends," he said as he hopped up the porch steps.

"Who are you calling old?" Katie teased him.

"I meant to say it's the sound of *gut* friends," Fletcher clarified. "*Gut* friends and *gut* women."

"For that, you may have the last doughnut." Tessa passed him a cream-filled pastry.

As Fletcher chewed, he noticed how reserved Anna seemed. She had dark circles under her eyes and he hoped he hadn't exhausted her with yesterday's activities. Or was there another reason she appeared fatigued? What happened after he left the previous evening? Did she remember something? Was it about Aaron? Determined not to let his dread get the best of him, he wiped his lips with the back of his hand and stood up.

"May I take you home, Anna?" he asked. "I know your family must have had a full buggy this morning."

"*Jah, denki*, Fletcher," she answered formally. "*Mach's. Gut.* Ka-tie. And. Tes-sa," she said slowly, and for some reason, this elicited peals of laughter from the Fisher sisters.

"Why did you use a funny voice when you said goodbye to Katie and Tessa?" Fletcher asked conversationally as they rode away.

"It was a private joke," was Anna's terse reply.

"Oh, I understand," Fletcher said, although

usually Anna enjoyed sharing her funny stories with him.

"*Jah*, I figured you might, since you like to keep certain matters private yourself," she replied stiffly.

Now Fletcher knew something was wrong. He jerked the reins, causing the horse to detour down a gravelly side road overlooking a meadow where stubbles of crocuses, tulips and wildflowers were beginning to poke through the rich soil.

When they stopped, he said, "If there's something troubling you, Anna, I wish you'd tell me outright."

"Ha!" she declared. "You're one to talk, considering what you haven't told me!"

"I honestly have no idea what you're referring to."

"I'm referring to the one very important, very personal thing you neglected to tell me!" Anna harrumphed, crossing her arms over her chest.

Fletcher was utterly baffled. Was the issue that was upsetting Anna now the same issue that caused her to write the note? "I'm sorry, but I still don't know what you're talking about."

"I'm talking about your first fiancée," she said, staring straight ahead.

Fletcher noticed he'd curled his fingers into a fist. The mention of Joyce always caused him to tense up. He loosely shook his hands and then rested them on his knees. "What about her?"

"Then you don't deny you were engaged to someone else before me?"

Fletcher snickered. "Of course I don't deny it. I told you all about her shortly after we first met."

Anna wasn't satisfied. "Perhaps, but why didn't you tell me about her after my accident?" she pressed. "You knew I wouldn't have remembered hearing about her."

Fletcher's temper flared, imagining how Anna might have learned about his first engagement. "Who has been telling you about these things from my past anyway? Was it Aaron? Melinda?" he guessed. "Or did you find your diary and read something there?"

"The question isn't who told me about your past, Fletcher. The question is why didn't *you* tell me about it?"

"It didn't seem important," he stated.

"Not important?" she challenged. "How can you say being engaged isn't important?"

She was sobbing into her hands now, and Fletcher recalled Dr. Donovan's concern about unprovoked emotional outbursts. He was worried that this might qualify. Then he realized that if it did, he also probably needed to consult a doctor because he felt disproportionately emotional, too. He had to calm down himself if he was going to be a comfort to Anna.

"Anna," he said, nudging her shoulder with his. "I didn't tell you about my allergy to mushrooms, either. Now *that* was important, but I didn't bring it up because at the time, it didn't seem relevant. That's the phrase I should have used. My first engagement didn't seem relevant."

Anna's giggle reassured Fletcher there was no need to seek medical attention: her tears had nothing to do with her concussion. His mind eased, he offered her a handkerchief, and soon her sniffing had quieted and she'd dabbed her cheeks dry.

"I'm sorry," she apologized and carefully folded the handkerchief into a triangle, ashamed to face him. "I didn't sleep a wink last night, but even so, that wasn't a very mature way for me to approach this topic."

"I should be more understanding," Fletcher acknowledged. "I can't imagine what it feels like to lose your memory."

"It feels like the sky looks," Anna said, pointing to the white, overcast expanse. "It feels vast and empty and colorless. I want to remember, but when I try, there's nothing there."

"Then it's up to me to do a better job of filling in the blanks," Fletcher stated firmly. "Joyce

Beiler was the name of my first fiancée. We courted for a year and although in hindsight I wouldn't say we were in love, I did care deeply for her and believed she felt the same way about me. Anyway, the summer before we decided to get married, Joyce's brother-in-law's cousin, Frederick, came to live with him and Joyce's sister, to help with growing and harvest seasons. I thought it was only natural that Joyce spent a lot of time with Frederick, since she was responsible for helping her sister and brother-in-law at the farm, too."

Noticing Fletcher's voice drop, Anna said softly, "It's okay, you needn't explain. I think I understand what happened."

But Fletcher cleared his throat and continued talking. "Eventually, I had a conversation—I had *several* conversations—with Joyce about my concerns, but she assured me she felt nothing but a sisterly type of fondness for Frederick. She and I completed our meetings with the deacon and announced our wedding intentions to our families and to the *leit* in church. Four days before the wedding, she told me she couldn't go through with it—she was in love with Frederick."

Anna gasped and touched Fletcher's forearm. "Oh! That must have been so painful for you."

"It was." He grimaced and hung his head. "At the time it felt personally excruciating and publicly disgraceful. I have to admit, I was relieved to leave Green Lake."

Anna understood only too well; Aaron's betrayal had wounded her deeply, too. But her relationship with Aaron hadn't progressed nearly as far as Fletcher's relationship had with Joyce, nor was the reason behind Anna's breakup public knowledge. She winced to imagine the extent of disbelief, disappointment and dejection—not to mention, embarrassment—Fletcher must have had to overcome, and her admiration for him burgeoned.

The air was silent except for the sound of the horse occasionally swishing his tail or shuffling his hooves, and after a few moments, Anna apologized. "I wish I hadn't made you relive that memory."

"It was necessary in order for me to clear it up with you," he replied. "I have nothing to hide so I don't want you to feel as if I'm keeping anything from you. I don't want you to feel as if there's something you need to keep from me, either. No matter what it is."

"Of course," Anna pledged pensively, noting the edge in Fletcher's tone. Did he think she was keeping something from him? If so, what? There was no other man in her life. The only person she'd ever walked out with was Aaron, and they'd broken up more than six months before Fletcher arrived in town. Since Fletcher was Anna's intended, she assumed she must have confided her intimate secrets to him, just as he'd confided his to her. That meant she must have told him what happened with Aaron and Melinda, didn't it? But, maybe she hadn't. Without asking, she couldn't be certain.

"What have I told you about my past?" Anna questioned.

Fletcher looked taken aback. "What do you mean?"

"I must have told you things about my life, but I can't remember what they are. What do you know about me?"

Fletcher wiped his upper lip. "Well, you told me about your *mamm* dying when you were a *bobbel* and how your *daed* and you lived with your *groossmammi* until she passed, too. I know that your *daed* married Naomi when you were sixteen, and it was a big adjustment for you to suddenly have four brothers around. You felt as if they were forever underfoot or spying on you."

Anna giggled. "Sometimes, I still feel that way about Eli and Evan."

"*Jah*, but you also said that helping Naomi care for them as young *kinner* made you eager to have *bobblin* of your own one day."

"What did I tell you about Melinda?"

Fletcher tilted his head from side to side, as if to work a kink out of his neck, before he said, "You said her *daed* sent her to stay with you because she was getting into trouble during her running-around period. He thought you might be a *gut* influence on her, since her *mamm* died long ago and she hadn't any female relatives living nearby."

"Go on," she prompted him.

"You tried to set a *gut* example and invited her to attend social events with you and Aaron, whom you'd been walking out with for about two and a half years. But then last February, you discovered Melinda and Aaron, um…"

Anna concluded his sentence for him, "Kissing behind the stable."

"Jah," Fletcher acknowledged.

"Did I tell you how I felt about that?"

"How you felt?" he repeated hesitantly. "Anna, are you sure you want to relive this?"

"I have no need to relive it—I already distinctly remember that part of my life. It happened long before my accident. What I want is to know what I told you about it. As your betrothed, I must have confided my innermost secrets in you. What did I tell you?" she challenged.

"You told me you were devastated at first, of course. But you said you soon realized it wasn't that Aaron had broken your heart as much as he'd broken your trust that pained you. Compared with losing your *daed*, you said ending your courtship with Aaron was easy. That's how you knew you hadn't truly been in love with him—because losing Aaron didn't split your heart in half."

"That's right." Anna nodded, contented to confirm Fletcher knew exactly how she felt. "What else did I tell you about the months following the breakup and my *daed*'s death?"

Fletcher's voice was gentle with compassion. "You told me spring was a blur. That everyone said how strong you were in the wake of your *daed*'s passing, caring for Naomi and the boys and putting up with Melinda's antics besides. You told me your secret was that you made yourself numb and kept as busy as you could. You said the only thing you looked forward to was the half hour you allowed yourself each day to weep in private—in the hayloft during the spring, and then beneath the willow by the creek in the warmer summer months. Which, as I've indicated, is where we first met."

Anna's eyes smarted. *I must have trusted him wholeheartedly to confide those emotions in him,* she realized.

Aloud, she said in a raspy voice, "*Denki* for

telling me all that. It helps me to know we've both shared our feelings and experiences so openly."

"Of course," Fletcher replied. Although time would tell if she'd come to remember she hadn't quite been open about sharing *all* of her feelings, he was grateful for the sense of calm that seemed to have settled over Anna. He wouldn't have forgiven himself if she'd gotten so upset they needed to call Dr. Donovan.

"Melinda told me I've seemed prickly since my accident," Anna said, interrupting his thoughts. "I don't mean to be that way, but it's frustrating trying to make sense of things. So I'll probably continue to ask you a lot of questions."

"Please do. As I said, we spent our early courting days down by the creek, just talking. We told each other all about our dreams and disappointments, our triumphs and our failures. We used to spend hours talking about our faith and our families, and we shared other details from our lives, too. For example, I even know that when you were a girl, you believed lightning bugs were actually made out of lightning."

"You mean they're not?" Anna laughed before requesting, "Now tell me some little thing I know about you that I don't know I know about you."

Relieved to engage in a little levity after such

an intense discussion, Fletcher pushed up his coat sleeve and lifted his arm. "See this scar? You know that I got it hurtling over a fence."

"Who was chasing you?"

"It wasn't a *who*, it was a *what*. It was Thistle, the neighbor's goat, to be precise."

"Ach! The mischievous animal!"

"Actually, I was the one who was mischievous. I was taking a shortcut, which amounted to trespassing. My first and last time."

"How old were you?"

"Oh, around twenty-two," Fletcher said.

"Neh!" Anna exclaimed. "Really?"

"Neh," he admitted. "Not really. I was about eight or nine. Definitely old enough to know better."

Laughing, Anna asked, "Did I confess any of my wayward escapades to you?"

"Only that you once burned your finger snatching an oatmeal cookie from your *groossmammi*'s oven. And that you used to climb trees to hide on your brothers."

"I still do that sometimes."

"Really?" Fletcher questioned.

"Neh, not really," Anna echoed impishly. "I'd like to think my behavior is a little more mature than that now. Although I haven't forgotten how to climb so I still could if I wanted to."

"Perhaps in warmer weather, you'll teach me,

then," Fletcher suggested, caught up in their whimsical banter. "That's one skill I never mastered. I have a slight fear of heights, which isn't one of the best qualities in a carpenter, so please don't tell Melinda. I don't want Aaron finding out about it and giving me a hard time. On the job, I do whatever needs to be done, including roofing—but how I feel about doing it is our little secret."

"I won't tell a soul, especially not Melinda," Anna agreed conspiratorially. "I don't think she intends any harm, but she has a habit of blurting things out before she's really thought them through."

"I've noticed that, too," Fletcher said. "Not only does she seem to share things she shouldn't, but half the time her perspective isn't exactly reliable."

"Is that why we were so discreet about our relationship, because we didn't want her to tell everyone and share her thoughts on the matter?" Anna wondered aloud.

"That was one of the reasons, I suppose," Fletcher confirmed. "I had similar misgivings about Aaron finding out. It was also that you wanted to be respectful of Naomi's mourning period. I think you felt a little guilty for being so happy when…"

"When my *daed* had recently died?"

"*Jah*. But there were a few people who knew we were courting early on, before we officially told our families."

"Who?"

"Well, Tessa and Katie. And my *groossdaadi*. Mind you, I never told him myself. He just knew. After you'd visit, he'd say, 'Fletcher, your Anna makes the best beef barley soup I've tasted since your *groossmammi* was alive.' Or, 'Your Anna's eyes were sure sparkling today, weren't they, Fletcher?' It was always 'your Anna,' not just 'Anna.' We never discussed it, but I think that was his way of letting me know he knew we were courting and he approved."

"I'm glad—on both counts," Anna said, rubbing her hands together.

The tip of her nose was pink and Fletcher's heartbeat quickened as he regarded the brightness of her lips, recalling how silky they used to feel against his own.

Her voice cut through his thoughts. "I'm afraid I'm getting a little chilly."

"Me, too," he said reluctantly. He picked up the reins and directed the horse back onto the roadway so he could drop Anna off and head toward his own house. The rhythmic cadence of the horse's clopping along the road made his eyelids droop and he decided that when he got home, he'd lie down for a much needed nap.

After stabling the horse, he realized he'd had such a full day with Anna on Saturday that he'd neglected to collect the mail that evening. Checking the box, he found an envelope addressed in penmanship he didn't immediately recognize. He quickly read its contents.

Fletcher,

We've received the invitation to your wedding from Anna, along with the note from you asking us to be your newehockers. We already have our suits from the last time you almost got married, so how could we say no?

In all sincerity, we're both glad you found a good woman and we look forward to meeting her and celebrating your marriage.

We expect to arrive on Monday, the sixth of April.

Your friends,

Chandler Schlabach & Gabriel Ropp.

In the turmoil following Anna's accident, Fletcher had forgotten he'd asked Chandler and Gabriel to be his *newehockers*. Recalling how supportive they'd been after his wedding debacle with Joyce, he knew their reference to it was intended lightly, and he was grateful he had friends who'd gladly make such a long journey on his behalf. Still, the remark touched upon his concerns that this wedding might not happen, either.

Yet as his head sunk into the pillow, he was cautiously upbeat as he reflected on the discussion he'd just had with Anna. Simply repeating what she'd told him about her breakup with Aaron made Fletcher feel more confident. Nothing about Anna's comments or behavior, past or present, indicated she held any enduring affection for his cousin. Fletcher still didn't know what to make of Anna's note, but maybe it was time for him to stop worrying about it. Perhaps the note only represented a single moment of hesitation, compared to an entire courtship of certainty. Could it be that today's conversation with Anna was further proof that there was nothing the two of them couldn't work out together if they talked it through? As Isaiah suggested, the best course of action might be to spend as much time with Anna as he could. *To know me is to love me*, he thought drowsily.

His mind made up, Fletcher felt more relaxed than he had since Anna's accident and he drifted into a languorous snooze.

Chapter Six

The house appeared to be deserted when Anna entered it, but she knew from experience that even if Melinda and the boys were out, it was likely Naomi was resting in her room. Tiptoeing down the hall, Anna hoped her stepmother wasn't relapsing into a period of depression and fatigue. If Naomi was sleeping, she didn't wish to rouse her, but if she was awake, Anna hoped she could be of some comfort.

"Are you asleep?" she asked quietly as she paused outside the closed bedroom door.

"I'll be right there," her stepmother called and Anna heard the patter of footsteps followed by what sounded like a drawer closing. When Naomi opened the door, her face was flushed. "Oh, *gut*, it's you, Anna."

"I'm sorry to disturb you. I wanted to see if

you were alright and if there's anything I can do for you."

"Anna, dear, you're always so considerate of me, but I'm fine," Naomi said. She stepped aside and motioned Anna into the bedroom. "Actually, I was in here looking for some fabric. Mind you, I wasn't sewing on the Sabbath—I was only looking to assess what I might have left over. I wanted to make new trousers for Raymond, as I've let down the hems in his church pants as far as they'll go and today I noticed they're still too short. I remembered starting a pair for your *daed* that I never finished. I'd tucked the material away until I could face seeing it again. While I was searching for it today, I found this. I'd forgotten all about it..."

She opened the bottom drawer of her bureau and removed a thick, neatly folded bundle of eggplant-colored fabric.

"Oh! That would be such a becoming color on you, Naomi," Anna replied, fingering the material. "Are you going to make yourself a new dress?"

Naomi's eyes shimmered. "I haven't sewn a dress for myself in so long, I've forgotten my measurements!"

"Then it's past time for you to have one."

Naomi laughed. "That's exactly the kind of remark your *daed* would have made, Anna."

"Well, he would have been right. Anyway, now that you've found the material, it would be wasteful to allow it to continue to sit in the drawer."

"You know what?" Naomi asked, patting the fabric. "I think I *will* make a new dress for myself. A wedding is such a special occasion and I'll wear the dress again to church for years."

Naomi's exuberance delighted Anna. In the past when her stepmother mentioned Anna's *daed*, she sounded so forlorn but today she conveyed only a sense of mirth and anticipation for the future, and her hopefulness felt contagious. Naomi set the material atop her sewing basket and the two women ambled into the kitchen for a cup of tea.

"Where are the boys this afternoon?" Anna asked.

"The four of them loped off to the creek. Roy and Raymond wanted to practice their casting and Eli and Evan tagged along for the fun of it. They were all hoping Fletcher might *kumme* down and join them for a while, too."

"He would have enjoyed that, but he left after he dropped me off."

Naomi narrowed her eyes. "Is something the matter? I assumed he'd stay for supper. We're only having leftovers because it's the Sabbath, but I figure our leftovers are tastier than whatever he might make on his own."

"*Neh*, nothing's wrong," Anna assured her. "I think he didn't want to wear out his *wilkom*, that's all."

"Ach! That's because I was so cranky the other night, isn't it? I didn't mean to be inhospitable, but I was short-tempered because of Melinda's comments. The truth is, both she and Aaron seem to be lacking in diligence. I think if they spent less time frolicking and more time tending to their responsibilities at home, instead of just those at their paid jobs, they'd have a better idea of what it means to manage a household. But it wasn't charitable of me to chase Aaron away as I did and I certainly wasn't hinting that Fletcher should go, too."

"I doubt Fletcher thought twice about leaving when he did," Anna replied. "As it was, I think he was surprised to be invited for supper since he'd already had dinner with us. He wouldn't take advantage of your generosity—he's very considerate in general."

"*Jah*, but I want you both to know he has an open invitation to join us for dinner or supper whenever he pleases. I know how important it is for the two of you to…to get to know each other again."

"*Denki*, Naomi, I'll tell him that," Anna said

as she lifted the whistling kettle from the front burner of the gas stove. "I have my follow-up doctor's appointment Tuesday afternoon, which he intends to take me to. It would be convenient if he could eat with us that evening, since we'll be returning home around five thirty or six o'clock."

"Of course," Naomi agreed, arranging several thimble cookies on a plate. "So, have you learned anything else about him other than that he's 'very considerate in general'?"

Anna carried the teacups to the table. Although she and Naomi shared an unusual closeness, most Amish couples in their district seldom discussed their romantic relationships.

"Well," she said, hesitating. Then her face broke into a huge grin. "I think the most important thing I've discovered is the more I know him, the more I like him."

"Look at you blush," Naomi gushed. "That's *wunderbaar.* Then do you still plan to marry him even if your memories don't fully return by your wedding date?"

"Oh, I haven't given up hope that my memories will *kumme* back!"

"That's what I'm praying will happen, too, and I have faith *Gott* will answer our prayers in His time and in His way."

Anna pensively bit into a cookie. After she

swallowed, she said, "I guess at this point—without having my memories restored—I'd say I might not be ready to marry Fletcher yet, but I can clearly see he has the qualities I'd want in a husband." She was referring to his fortitude and candor, and to how respectful, protective and understanding he'd shown himself to be.

"And are you drawn to him?"

"Drawn to him?" Anna repeated, drizzling honey into her tea.

"A number of men might have the qualities you'd desire in a husband, but they don't set your heart aflutter," Naomi stated candidly.

Anna thought of how her heart melted within—like honey in tea—whenever Fletcher's eyes met hers. *"Jah,"* she said, "I'm drawn to him."

"Then it sounds as if you just need a little more time," Naomi suggested.

"Or for my memories to return," Anna replied, frowning. "Although I'd settle for finding my journal. As fond as I'm growing of Fletcher, I'm still surprised I made the decision to marry him so quickly."

"It's wise to know someone well before committing to marriage, but knowing someone well doesn't necessarily mean having a long courtship," Naomi reasoned. "I only knew your *daed* for four months before I married him. I had a solid sense of his character from the first day I met him and that never changed. I loved your *daed* early on and I knew he loved me. We were meant for each other. There was no other way to explain it and no other explanation needed."

Anna kissed Naomi's forehead as she stood to bring the empty teacups to the sink. "I'm so blessed you and my *daed* got married, Naomi. I'm sorry for how cross I acted that first year because I had to give up my bedroom to Raymond and Roy."

Naomi laughed. "You've more than made up for it by sharing your room with Melinda so graciously." Then, in a serious tone, she said, "I must admit I hoped—even prayed—Melinda and Aaron might have second thoughts about getting married. I think they both could benefit from maturing a little individually before they begin a life together as husband and wife."

"Well, as you've been reminding me, there's still time…"

Anna's comments were disrupted by the sound of footsteps on the porch as the four boys burst through the mudroom into the kitchen.

"Don't worry, *Mamm*, Evan's fine, he's just wet," Raymond immediately announced as he placed his soggy brother down on the floor.

"And cold," Evan said, shivering.

"Haven't we had enough accidents in this family? Didn't I warn you to keep a close eye on him?" Naomi upbraided Raymond and Roy as she rushed Evan to the washroom for a hot bath.

As Anna pulled plates from the cupboard to set the table for supper, she couldn't help but think that if Fletcher had gone fishing with the boys, he would have snatched Evan out of the creek before the boy had a chance to get wet. Because not only did Fletcher have the most striking eyes she'd ever gazed into, but Anna noticed he had particularly strong arms, too.

On Monday morning, Raymond delivered a note to Fletcher from Anna. *Fletcher,* it said, *would you like to join us for supper? I'm making meat loaf and brown-butter mashed potatoes, with butterscotch cream pie for dessert. Naomi wanted to be sure you know you are* wilkom *to join us. —Anna.*

Fletcher's mouth watered at the thought of Anna's cooking, but he had to decline. He had to work late in order to make up for the time he'd miss the next day when he left early to take Anna to Highland Springs. As it was, he, Aaron, Raymond and Roy would have to struggle to keep up with their contracts. The trim Aaron ordered for the first site wasn't delivered that morning, so Aaron suggested they temporarily abandon the location to begin working on the new project at a second site. Fletcher was concerned the first customer would be upset by the delay in the completion of the assignment, but Aaron shrugged it off.

"It's unfortunate, *jah*, but when I explain to the customer that our supplier hasn't delivered the trim yet, he'll understand," Aaron said. "The *Englisch* crews are usually much farther behind their deadlines than we are, so the customer won't think twice about it."

Fletcher had gritted his teeth. Aaron was a good carpenter, but he lacked the kind of drive and the organizational skills his father possessed. If Isaiah had been managing this project, he would have seen to it the supplies were ordered ahead of time.

"Perhaps, but our purpose is to honor our word and bring glory to *Gott*, not merely to do better than our *Englisch* competitors," he reminded his cousin.

"If you're so worried about it, tonight you can stop at the lumber store after you're done making up your time and ask the clerk to expedite the order. I've also made a list of supplies we need for our next job. Most of it is small enough to load into your buggy. The rest they can deliver with the trim."

"How will I pay for it?" Fletcher asked.

"Here, take the card. Just sign the receipt 'Chupp,' like you usually do."

Fletcher knew he was the only crew member Aaron entrusted with this task, but it wasn't a job Fletcher appreciated being assigned. The purchasing of supplies was usually the foreman's responsibility. Fletcher was only willing to do it because it would expedite progress on their customers' projects. It wasn't until later in the evening, when he was alone, wolfing down a cheese and bologna sandwich, that it dawned on Fletcher what the real reason was Aaron tasked him with visiting the lumber store that evening: Aaron didn't want go himself because he feared he'd miss the opportunity to be invited to Melinda's house for supper. In fact, he was probably devouring a thick slice of Anna's meat loaf at that very moment.

Fletcher relished Anna's cooking, knowing the satisfaction she took in providing healthful, tasty meals for her family, her friends or *leit* in the church who happened to be visiting or ailing. Yet he realized even she needed a break from her responsibilities from time to time, and he decided he'd like to treat her to supper out after her doctor's appointment. It would be a surprise—a good one, for once.

The very thought carried him through his work that evening and the following day, and before he knew it, he was knocking at her door. Knowing Naomi would fret if he and Anna were late returning from the medical center, but anticipating he might not be able to speak to Naomi in private, Fletcher carried a folded note. *Naomi,* it read, *I'd like to surprise Anna by taking her out for dinner after her appointment. We may not be returning until later in the evening. Is that okay with you? —Fletcher.*

When Anna went to retrieve her shawl, Fletcher slipped Naomi the note and gestured for her to read it. She quickly scanned the slip of paper and crumpled it in her fist just as Anna came back into the room. With a wink at Fletcher, Naomi bid them goodbye. They were about to board the buggy when she called from the porch, "Be careful and have an *appenditlich* time, you two!"

Waving back at her, Anna asked Fletcher, "What do you think she meant by that?"

Fletcher recalled the time he told Anna she smelled *appenditlich* and his cheeks burned. Avoiding her question as he assisted her into the buggy, he advised, "Watch your step."

The sunlight played off the trees, which waved their branches in a light breeze, and the landscape was beginning to blossom with azaleas, crocuses and daffodils. As Fletcher and Anna passed them, he recognized how much more buoyant he was during this trip than he'd been the last time he'd taken Anna to Highland Springs, and he hummed a few measures of the hymn they'd sung in church on Sunday.

"How are you feeling, Anna?" Dr. Donovan asked when he entered the exam room.

"Wunderbaar," Anna answered in Pennsylvania Dutch. She quickly clarified, for the doctor's benefit, "I mean, wonderful."

Dr. Donovan's round cheeks grew even rounder when he chuckled. "Even if I hadn't known what you meant by the word *wunderbaar*, I could have guessed by the color in your cheeks and the glint in your eye. *Wunderbaar* is a big improvement from *fine*, isn't it?"

"It is," Anna agreed.

After questioning her about any ongoing nausea or headaches, he told her to hop onto the examining table, where he looked into her eyes and quickly tested her reflexes before telling her to take a seat in the chair next to Fletcher again.

"Physically, you're in great shape," the doctor reported. "I'm glad to hear the nausea has subsided. The dull headaches you mentioned are probably a sign you're doing a bit more focused concentrating than you ought to be doing. Have you been heeding my advice not to do too much sewing or reading?"

"Oh, I haven't been reading at all," Anna stated with a wide-eyed innocent look.

"Aha!" Dr. Donovan pointed his finger in mock accusation, grinning. "You'll need to cut back on sewing, then. I'd advise that you don't return to your job at the shop yet, either. Now, how about your memories, have they returned yet?"

Anna shook her head. "Not yet."

"Hmm," the doctor murmured thoughtfully. "Well, they still might. Although, as I said before, there's no guarantee. But something tells me the two of you may have gotten reacquainted, perhaps rediscovered some of the qualities in each other that made you fall in love in the first place. Am I right?"

Anna modestly dipped her head so Fletcher answered for them both, saying, "We've enjoyed spending time together recently, *jah*."

"Wunderbaar!" Dr. Donovan exclaimed, smacking his desktop, and Anna and Fletcher both laughed. "Have faith and keep heading forward and things will turn out alright, one way or the other."

While Anna was scheduling an appointment to return in four weeks, Fletcher went to retrieve the buggy from the lot. After picking her up, he skillfully maneuvered the horse through the heavy traffic along the main road. Oddly feeling as skittish as he did the first time he formally asked to court her, he didn't speak until they turned down a side street.

"If you're hungry, I'd like to take you to supper," he said.

"*Denki*, that's a very nice invitation," Anna replied slowly, as if considering the offer, "but Naomi will grow concerned if we're not back by six or six thirty."

"It's okay, I cleared it with her first," Fletcher confessed.

"Really? You're so thoughtful!" Anna said, clasping her hands and shuffling her feet. "Is there a special place we've frequented?"

"*Neh*. We've never actually eaten out together, but I think it's time to do something new to both of us, not just new to you. Don't you agree?"

"I'd like that," Anna said and Fletcher stared into her eyes so long a driver from behind tapped on his horn to indicate the signal light had turned green.

They chose to dine at a pizza place Anna had heard some *Englisch* customers rave about in Schrock's Shop, and the food lived up to the recommendation. Together Anna and Fletcher polished off a medium Hawaiian pizza as well as a pitcher of root beer, which gave Anna hiccups that lasted all the way home.

"*Gut nacht*, Fletcher," she said when he

walked her to her door. "I *hic*—had an absolutely *scrumptious* time. *Hic*."

By the time he turned in for the night, Fletcher's jaw ached from grinning but he still couldn't stop smiling. Their evening out seemed to underscore what Dr. Donovan suggested: Anna and Fletcher needed to move forward, not backward. They needed to have faith and to focus on the future, not on the past. As the doctor said, there was no guarantee Anna's memory would ever return. If not, she wouldn't ever be able to tell him what she'd meant when she sent her note the day of her accident. But since nothing about her actions or attitude indicated any special affinity for Aaron, Fletcher decided it was time to put the note behind him for good. He turned off the lamp and floated into sleep.

On Wednesday, Anna woke to the thrumming of rain on the rooftop and the low rumble of distant thunder, which struck her as odd. It seemed early in the season for thunder. The last storm they had was in October, on Fletcher's birthday. She lay there thinking about how upset she'd been when the cloudburst ruined her carefully planned picnic beneath the willow at the creek. Making a dash for Fletcher's buggy, she'd tripped on a tree root, stumbling face-first toward the ground. When Fletcher lunged to catch her, he'd dropped the basket he'd been carrying, upending its contents beside her. They both ended up splattered with cake and mud. She wondered how she ever explained her appearance to her family that day.

Then she sat bolt upright in bed: she had remembered something from the last six months!

She tucked her hair into her prayer *kapp* and knelt by her bed. "Dear Lord, *denki* for restoring my memory. *Denki, denki, denki!*"

"Shh," Melinda groaned. "I can't take a nap in the middle of the day like you can and I still need to sleep."

"But I remembered! I remembered!" Anna said, shaking her cousin's shoulders. When she elicited no further response, she dressed and hopped down the stairs and into the kitchen.

"I remembered something!" she announced, hugging Naomi, who was standing at the stove scrambling eggs.

"*Gott* is *gut*," Naomi proclaimed, dropping her wooden spoon to take Anna's face in her hands. "See? It just took time."

"Why are you two crying?" Raymond asked when he entered the room.

Anna leaped to hug him. "Because *Gott* is *gut*!"

"What's all the noise? Is there a party going on in here?" Roy asked a few seconds later.

"Not yet, but there will be tonight, if your *mamm* allows it," Anna said. "We'll invite Fletcher, Aaron, Katie and Tessa for supper and a cake. I'll buy the ingredients and do all of the work myself, I promise."

"Anna, you know what the doctor said about overexertion—"

"He only warned me about up close activities. Besides, it won't be any different than preparing a meal for our family—it will just be a bigger meal. If I truly need help, Katie and Tessa will pitch in," Anna countered. "I had a great sleep last night and I'm obviously getting better or else I wouldn't have experienced one of my memories returning."

Eli rubbed his eyes as he took his seat. "Your memory came back?"

"Now maybe you'll remember what happened to Timothy!" Evan added, picking up a fork.

"It was only a single memory and it wasn't about your turtle, Evan, but it's still a cause for celebration."

"*Jah*, okay," Naomi agreed. "As long as you don't overdo it."

"*Denki,*" Anna said. "I'll drop Melinda off, so I can go to the market. She can invite Tessa and Katie when she sees Tessa at work. They'll probably give her a ride home, too. Raymond, I'll give you a note to give to Fletcher. But whatever anyone does, you mustn't let him know I started to remember again—even after he arrives here. I have an idea for how I want to surprise him with the news. So, mum's the word, right, Eli and Evan?"

"Right," said Evan, pretending to seal his lips shut. Then out of one corner of his mouth, he squeaked, "I won't say a word."

"You'd better not," Eli warned. "Terrible things happen when you spy or share other people's secrets."

"I don't know if that's true," Anna commented as she searched a drawer for a piece of paper. She and Naomi were concerned about Melinda's influence on the younger boys, so they'd been trying to teach Eli and Evan the value of discretion, but Anna wondered if they'd been too strict on the subject. "I would just appreciate it if we kept this a secret. This way, we'll all have the pleasure of seeing the surprised look on Fletcher's face!"

Dearest Fletcher, she wrote on a piece of paper. *Please come to supper tonight at six. You will like what I am making. —Your Anna.* Sealing the note with a piece of tape, she instructed Raymond to give it to Fletcher as soon as he got to the work site.

"And please tell Aaron he's invited, too," she added, knowing that when Melinda finally dragged herself from bed, she'd be as pleased about her fiancé joining them for supper as Anna was about hers.

Fletcher began whistling the moment after reading Anna's message. It wasn't just that he was happy he'd get to see her again this evening; it was that she used not one but *two* terms of endearment in her note. Even before her accident, she was careful about what she expressed to him in writing. She said she trusted Raymond not to read her messages, but she wasn't as certain she always trusted him to remember to deliver the notes and she didn't want her "sweet nothings" ending up in someone else's hands by accident.

He was still whistling when he, Raymond and Roy packed up their tools for the day. Despite the fact that Aaron had left early to go to the lumber store again, they were managing to keep on schedule with their new project. Anna's *daed* had trained the boys well. They were hard workers and applied whatever techniques he taught them. Raymond was already nearly as handy of a carpenter as Aaron was, and what he lacked in skill, he made up for in perseverance.

"It's rainy, getting dark and there's a lot of traffic. Roy, you need more practice," Fletcher instructed, handing the boy the reins.

Roy gladly accepted the responsibility and

soon they were situating Fletcher's buggy next to Tessa and Katie's at the Weavers' house. As Fletcher was hitching the horse to the post, Aaron arrived.

"Looks like quite a gathering," Fletcher remarked, pulling a carrot from a sack he kept for the animal. "It should be a pleasant evening."

"*Jah*, provided Anna doesn't sicken anyone with her cooking tonight." Aaron laughed. "Although Katie Fisher probably eats the most, so she's in the greatest danger."

Fletcher didn't know whether Aaron's remarks were intended to be as derisive as they sounded or if they were only another misguided attempt at humor. "I wish you wouldn't talk about Anna or her friends like that. Or anyone else, for that matter," he said. "Some of your remarks aren't funny. They're unkind."

"If I'm so unkind and unfunny, why did Anna date me for almost three years?" Aaron asked as water dripped off the brim of his hat. Then he answered his own question. "She dated me because she liked me."

Surprised but undaunted by his cousin's bluster, Fletcher lifted his chin and straightened his posture. "And yet, she's marrying *me*," he said defiantly.

"Only because I chose to walk out with Melinda instead," Aaron challenged. He patted his horse on the flank before adding, "And whether or not Anna marries you is yet to be seen." Then he strode toward the house.

Fletcher removed his hat and looked toward the sky, allowing the rain to cool both his skin and his temper before he joined the others inside. *Please, Lord, forgive me my anger. Give me patience and bless our fellowship tonight.*

"*Denki*, Naomi, for having me over again," he said after he'd removed his muddy boots and was standing in the kitchen.

"This is all Anna's doing," Naomi explained, "but you're always *wilkom*, Fletcher."

As Anna glided into the room, he noticed her eyes were luminous and her creamy complexion was tinged with pink. He sensed something about her had changed. Rather, something was very much the same as it used to be. He didn't know exactly what it was, but the width of her smile was accentuated by the sincerity of her tone when she said, "Hello, Fletcher. I'm very glad to see you again."

After they were seated, said grace and filled their plates with creamed chicken, noodles and chow chow, Katie complimented Anna. "This chicken is so yummy. You've done something different with the recipe, haven't you?"

To Fletcher's consternation, Aaron butted in,

spouting, "*Jah*, she left all of the poisonous ingredients out this time."

Before Fletcher could defend Anna, she was gripped with paroxysms of laughter and then Eli and Evan were, too. Their laughter was so infectious it wasn't long before Katie and Tessa were clutching their sides, although they had no idea why, so Anna recounted the incident, with the younger boys performing an exaggerated re-enactment that included Fletcher's eyes bulging before he fainted to the floor, gasping for air.

Whether Anna realized it or not, her ability to turn something that was intended as a barb into a source of amusement was one of her former qualities he deeply appreciated, and Fletcher chuckled in spite of himself. The rest of the meal was also accentuated by spirited conversation and peals of laughter. Afterward, Katie and Tessa cleared the dishes from the table while Anna prepared the dessert.

"Okay, now, Evan," she said to her youngest brother, who dimmed the lamp.

Fletcher didn't understand why until Anna turned from the counter balancing a large cake aglow with candles. *She looks so pretty*, he thought. *But I wonder whose birthday it is*.

"Happy birthday to you," Katie started to sing. Although he didn't know who they were singing to, Fletcher joined the others. He was surprised when Anna hovered near his shoulder and everyone sang, "Happy birthday, dear Fletcher, happy birthday to you."

"Denki," he said hesitantly when she placed the cake in front of him. He didn't want to embarrass her in front of everyone by telling her it wasn't his birthday.

"Make a wish and then blow them out," she instructed merrily.

As soon as he extinguished the candles, everyone burst into applause. When Naomi turned up the lamp again, he noticed the cake Anna had prepared was his favorite: turtle cake, a gooey, melt-in-your-mouth chocolate cake that included pecans, chocolate chips and caramel.

"This is a *wunderbaar* celebration!" he said, "I haven't had turtle cake since—"

"Since I made one for your actual birthday in October and you were carrying it and you tripped. We both ended up wearing it instead of eating it," Anna said, her eyes gleaming.

"That's right. You were so—" Fletcher began to speak but his mouth dropped open midsentence. "Anna! You remembered?"

She nodded and his heart palpitated. He was torn between feelings of absolute jubilance that Anna might begin to remember their courtship and utter despondency that she might also recall her hesitance to marry him.

"Stop catching flies," Aaron ribbed him. "Don't you have anything to say?"

"You remembered?" he asked again, quieter this time, staring into Anna's eyes.

"I remembered," she confirmed. "I still can't recall anything else from the past six months, but I definitely remember your last birthday."

"Are we going to get a piece of cake before his *next* birthday?" Roy interrupted and the others all laughed.

While they were devouring their cake, Fletcher's mind reeled. He could hardly concentrate on the anecdote Anna was sharing about his birthday picnic mishap, which kept everyone in stitches, especially when she got to the part about trying to salvage the cake from the puddle it landed in.

"I guess that's why they call it *turtle* cake," Evan punned.

"They're going to call *you* a turtle at school tomorrow if you stay up much later," Naomi said. "*Kumme*, it's time for you and Eli to get ready for bed."

Since Anna refused Tessa's and Katie's help with the remaining dishes, they bid their goodbyes. To Fletcher's surprise, Aaron gamely offered to walk them to their buggy.

"I'll *kumme*, too, since I have a flashlight," Melinda chimed in and followed them out the door.

As Fletcher was lacing his boots in the mudroom, Anna brought him the remainder of the turtle cake, which she had secured in waxed paper for him to take home.

"*Denki*, I will savor this," he said, although eating was the last thing on his mind.

"There's something else." She handed him a small package wrapped in bright green cellophane. "What's a birthday party without a present?"

He untied the silver bow and pulled out a round jar with a black top. "Honey and oatmeal salve," he read. "This is something I definitely need."

"It's the kind my *daed* always used. I noticed your hands are a bit dry, too. *Daed* often said if the floors he installed cracked as badly as his skin, he'd be out of work," she quoted. "Here, try it."

She unscrewed the lid and dipped her finger into the salve. After applying it to the back of his hand, she began caressing it into his skin in gentle circles. "Doesn't that feel better?" she asked, reaching for the jar again.

Agitated by her news and fearful she'd notice

his hand shaking, Fletcher pulled away, saying, "*Denki*, but it's getting late. I should go."

"Oh, okay," she said, quickly wiping her fingers on her apron.

The pained, perplexed look that crossed Anna's face rivaled Fletcher's aching inner turmoil. In bed that night, he shifted his body from side to side as his mind leaped from one thought to another. How long before Anna recalled what she meant by her note? Should he tell her about it before she remembered, or would that only upset her? And what about him? Could he really bear to know the truth, now that the past was no longer past?

Chapter Seven

On Thursday morning, Anna lay in bed, thinking about the previous evening. As euphoric as she was that her memories were starting to return, she simultaneously felt let down by Fletcher's subdued reaction. In response to her news, she had imagined a scenario in which he would have picked her up, twirled her around and declared there was no better "birthday" gift he could have received than having her memory come back. Instead, he hardly uttered a word about it and he noticeably flinched when she later took his hand in hers to soften it with salve.

Wasn't he a physically demonstrative person? Try as she did to recall, she couldn't summon any recollection of the two of them holding hands or embracing before her accident. After her accident, he'd occasionally offered his hand or arm to steady her, but not as a spontaneous gesture of affection. Perhaps his reticence was simply part of his personality. Or was he upset by something else? Had she done something to perturb him? Was he taken aback that she shared the story of his original birthday party with everyone else?

There was only one way to find out: talk to him. He'd indicated he wanted them to be open with each other, didn't he? That was her desire, too. Anna quickly rose, donned her *kapp* and thanked the Lord for the memory He'd restored and for those yet to come. Then she finished dressing, made her bed and tiptoed out of the room in order not to wake Melinda.

After making oatmeal with raisins for her brothers, she scribbled a quick note for Raymond to deliver to Fletcher. *My dear Fletcher*, she began, but then she feared he might think it sounded too coquettish. She ripped up the paper and started again. *Fletcher, will you join us for supper at six o'clock? There's something I'd like to discuss with you. —Anna.*

Aaron had arranged to pick Roy and Raymond up that morning, and as soon as his buggy departed the lane, Eli and Evan entered the kitchen.

"Eggs, oatmeal, or cinnamon raisin French toast, boys?" she asked them.

"French toast, please!" they chorused.

"How did I know?" Anna chuckled as she sliced the loaf of bread Naomi made the day before.

The boys sat quietly at the table, rubbing their eyes and chatting with Anna as she made their breakfast. She was glad her stepmother was catching a few extra minutes of sleep; she always relished spending time alone with Eli and Evan. When they were younger, she used to pretend they were her children, not Naomi's, and she suddenly realized how quickly they were growing and how much she'd miss their familiar childish expressions and antics.

"Have you remembered anything else, Anna?" Evan asked, stifling a yawn.

"*Neh*, not yet. But I trust it won't be long until everything returns to me, so if you've done anything naughty in the past six months that I never found out about, don't think you've gotten away with it!" she joked, kissing the tops of their blond heads as she reached over them to set the platter of French toast on the table.

"Don't worry," Evan said, shaking his head vigorously. "*Mamm* already reprimanded me for anything I did that I shouldn't have done!"

Anna had to pinch the skin on her wrist to keep from laughing so she could say grace. After she lifted her head, she picked up the serving fork and asked, "How many slices would you like, Eli?"

"I'm... I'm not hungry," Eli whimpered. "My stomach hurts."

"Your stomach hurts?" Naomi sounded alarmed as she entered the kitchen. Placing a hand on Eli's head, she said, "He doesn't seem hot to me. What do you think, Anna?"

Anna felt his forehead and then slid her hand down to his cheek. "*Neh*, he's not warm. But if you think he should stay home from school, I could—"

"I don't want to stay home from school," Eli insisted. "I'm just not hungry. May I be excused from the table?"

"Of course," Anna said. "Why don't you go lie down on the sofa and I'll fill a hot water bottle for your tummy? Evan and I will do your morning chores for you before school starts— how's that?"

"*Gut,*" the boy replied, shuffling out of the room.

"If he's too sick to eat, may I have his pieces of French toast?" Evan asked.

"*Neh*, we don't want you getting a tummy ache, too," Anna replied. "But you may have *one* additional piece, since you'll need extra energy to help me with his chores."

"*Denki*, Anna!" Evan said, leaning over his plate.

"Why are you smiling like that?" Anna whispered to Naomi above Evan's head. "Is it because of his appetite?"

"*Neh*, it's because of your aptitude. You're going to make a *wunderbaar mamm*."

Anna couldn't keep the bliss from her voice when she replied, "That's because I had you as my example."

"Some example I am—I almost slept as late as Melinda did today!" Naomi pointed to the window. "It's cloudy, but it's supposed to be warm again. I think I'll take advantage of the weather and begin some gardening today."

"While you're doing that, I'll wash the windows," Anna suggested.

"I don't know if that's wise. Did Dr. Donovan say it's okay to resume strenuous activities?"

"It's hardly strenuous. In fact, it gives my brain time to wander and that's when the memories seem likely to return."

Naomi reluctantly approved. "Well, the windows do need cleaning. I suppose if you take breaks, it might be alright. It will also give me time to work on preparing bedding arrangements for our guests' *kinner*. I'm thinking of putting all the boys on the second floor. Do you think it's warm enough for the girls to sleep in the attic room next to yours?"

"It will be if they're all tucked in side by side," Anna said.

Naomi's question reminded Anna that she needed to retrieve her new material from the other side of the attic and store it in her closet. She'd been helping Melinda with her dress so frequently that she hadn't taken her own fabric out of its wrapping, except to discreetly give Katie and Tessa their share of the material the evening before. Because she didn't want Naomi to hear her talk about sewing, Anna hadn't had the chance to ask her friends if they wanted to schedule a sister day to work on their dresses. Worried about whether they'd finish them on time, Anna thought, *Katie's a terrible procrastinator. A day before* Grischtdaag, *she still didn't even know what gifts she was going to give to her* mamm *and* daed.

It took a moment for Anna to realize she'd recalled another memory, and when she did, she was nearly as ecstatic as when it happened the first time. Throughout the day, additional remnants of the previous six months flitted through her mind. Her recollections were random and relatively minor—she recalled quilting with other women from the church, wading with the boys at the creek and the day an *Englisch* customer inquired about purchasing a dozen *kapps* in the shop. Many of the memories were fragmented and some were hazier than others, but there was no doubt her recollections were authentic, since no one had given her any hint about the events she recalled. She was so invigorated that she breezed through washing all of the windows in the house.

She was wringing out her rag after wiping the final pane when Evan and Eli returned from school and Melinda from the shop. Shortly afterward, as Anna was peeling potatoes for supper, she heard a buggy in the lane and had to restrain herself from throwing open the door to greet Fletcher. But it was Aaron who walked in with Roy. A minute later, Raymond followed, bearing a return message for her.

Anna, Fletcher wrote at the bottom of her own note to him, *I have to work late tonight and again tomorrow installing trim. Perhaps I can see you on Saturday? —Fletcher.*

Her eyes stung as she reread the note. Fletcher had told her how eager he was to complete the remaining trim for their first customer, so she understood why he needed to work late, but she was disappointed his message didn't contain so much as a jot of endearment or tittle of appreciation for the invitation. She supposed he could have simply been in a rush when he replied, but again she wondered if he was displeased with her. Or could it be he was tiring of eating at Naomi's with Anna's entire family?

Not knowing what to think, Anna penned a

simple response under Fletcher's signature: *I'll be doing housework and gardening, so I should be home if you stop by on Saturday*. There wasn't room left on the page for her full name, so she merely scrawled her first initial.

There, she thought. *That doesn't sound the least bit cloying, so he shouldn't feel obligated to visit*. But deep down, she hoped by Saturday afternoon Fletcher would be as eager to see her as she was to see him.

Fletcher couldn't shake his apprehension that any second now, Anna would recall whatever it was that had caused her to write the note on the day of her accident. He felt as if his temples were being compressed by a vise, and his persistent nausea was exacerbated by the messages Raymond delivered. The first one, which read, *there's something I'd like to discuss with you*, was reminiscent of her preaccident note, *I have a serious concern regarding A. that I must discuss privately with you*. The chilly tone of her second inscription further heightened his jitters.

He was actually relieved to have a valid excuse for turning down her supper invitation: the trim had finally been delivered for the first project and he wanted to hang it as soon as possible. Aaron wouldn't release him from the second customer's site during the day, claiming the trim could wait another week. As a matter of providing good service, however, Fletcher assured the first customer he'd hang the trim after hours, completing it by Friday evening.

By Saturday morning, however, Fletcher was so sleep-deprived, miserable and beside himself with agitation, he could hardly wait to talk to Anna about the topic he'd been dreading for so long. As devastating as he anticipated their discussion would be, he knew it was better to face the truth than to suffer the agony of waiting for the issue to come to light.

Bleary-eyed, he whacked his thumb with his hammer, a carelessness even Roy hadn't demonstrated after his first month on the job.

"Ouch!" he yelled and flung the hammer to the floor

"You need ice?" Raymond asked.

"I need air," Fletcher responded, heading out the door.

In the parking lot, he paced in circles, trying to shake off the pain. When it didn't subside, he took a short jaunt to the corner store to purchase three cups of coffee and what passed for glazed doughnuts in the *Englisch* community. Upon returning, he crossed paths with Aaron, who had just arrived to work and was hitching his horse.

"Where have you been?" Aaron asked.

Fletcher held up the tray of coffee to indicate

his response. "Where have you been?" he asked in return.

"Not that I have to answer to you, but I was assessing another project," Aaron said. "I told you once before, if you're going to change your schedule, you need to let me know. You shouldn't leave Roy and Raymond unsupervised at the work site."

"I didn't change my schedule," Fletcher explained, thrown off by Aaron's tone. "I was gone all of five minutes."

"Don't let it happen again," Aaron warned before helping himself to a cup of coffee from the tray and strutting away.

Fletcher kicked at the dirt. The throbbing in his thumb was nothing compared to the pounding in his head. *Please* Gott, *give me grace*, he prayed. *The grace to deal with Aaron's attitude and the grace to accept whatever Anna has to say this afternoon.*

His morning progressed without further injury and Fletcher was pleasantly surprised when Isaiah arrived midmorning and took him aside to thank him for finishing the trim at the other customer's site. After his shift ended, Fletcher stopped at home to change his shirt before traveling to Anna's house. The closer he drew, the drier his mouth grew and by the time he pulled into the yard, he felt as if his tongue were made of wool.

"Fletcher!" Evan beckoned from behind a tree near where Fletcher hitched his horse. "Don't tell Anna you saw me—we're playing hide-and-seek."

"Too late, Evan," Anna said, creeping up from behind and tagging him on the shoulder. "You're it!"

"Aww, alright," Evan moaned. "Fletcher can play, too."

"*Neh*, Fletcher and I are going to take a walk to the creek, aren't we, Fletcher?"

"*Jah,*" was all he could say.

Before ambling away, Anna instructed Evan, "After you find Eli, I'd like both of you to take that basket of laundry inside the house and wash your hands for dinner. Then ask your *mamm* if there's anything you can do to help her."

As she and Fletcher traipsed down the hilly field, they chatted about the spring birds they spotted, Fletcher's new project at work and Isaiah's visit to the site. Fletcher assumed Anna was stalling until they arrived at the creek before discussing her note, and with each step he felt as if he wore cinder blocks strapped to his feet.

When they reached the embankment, he viewed the rushing water and remembered a saying his sister Leah often quoted, "If the river had no rocks, it would not have a song."

"What?" Anna questioned.

Fletcher didn't realize he'd spoken aloud. "Oh, that's a proverb my sister often says. I think it means you can't have something beautiful without also having some rocky, difficult patches."

"That's true," Anna said, thoughtfully furrowing her brow.

Unable to endure the suspense any longer, Fletcher blurted out, "You mentioned there was something you wanted to speak with me about. What is it?"

Anna shuffled backward. "Let's sit," she said and they positioned themselves next to each other on a large boulder overlooking the water. "It's…it's uncomfortable to discuss this."

Fletcher licked his lips and forged ahead. "Whatever it is, it's better that we're open with each other about it."

"I guess I… I was disappointed by your reaction the other night when I told you my memory had begun to return. I thought you would have been happier," Anna confessed. "I thought you would have been thrilled, actually. When you weren't, I wondered why not. I wondered if I'd done something to upset you."

Fletcher closed his eyes as he absorbed the realization that Anna still didn't recall writing her original note. For a split second, he considered not telling her about his concern, but he knew he'd only be prolonging the inevitable. Besides, it had become too big of a burden for him to bear even a second longer.

"You're right, Anna. I probably didn't seem as excited as I should have been," he intoned. "That's because there's something about the past I've wanted to discuss with you, but I couldn't because Dr. Donovan warned us it would be detrimental to your health if you became too upset or if you felt too pressured to recall your memories before your brain had a chance to heal. But it's been weighing heavily on my mind and I can't keep it to myself any longer, especially since it affects our wedding."

Anna gasped and pressed a hand to her mouth before asking, "What is it?"

"It's this," he said, removing the slip of paper from his coat and shoving it into her hand.

She unfolded the note and read it aloud. "'Fletcher, I have a serious concern regarding A. that I must discuss privately with you before the wedding preparations go any further. Please visit me tonight after work. —Anna.'"

Then she read it again to herself. Finally, she said, "It's sloppier than usual, but it's definitely my handwriting. When did I give you this?"

"You sent it with Raymond the morning of your accident."

"Really? I'm sorry, but I have no recollection of what I wanted to talk to you about."

"I believe the A. stands for Aaron."

"Aaron? What does he have to do with our wedding preparations? He hasn't lifted a finger to help as far as I can tell, has he?"

"Neh." Fletcher grimaced. It was clear he was going to have to spell it out for Anna and his stomach lurched as he formed the words. "I believe you meant... You meant you had second thoughts about how you felt about him, so you had second thoughts about marrying me."

Anna hooted, "That's absurd!" She leaped up and twirled to face him with her hands on her hips. "How could you believe such a thing, especially after all the conversations we've had?"

"I don't want to believe it, but it's possible something happened immediately before the accident that caused you to change your mind about how you felt about Aaron and you just can't remember it."

"I might not remember all of what *happened* in the past six months, but I remember how I *felt* ever since breaking up with Aaron," Anna insisted, smacking the back of one hand against the palm of the other. "My *feelings* haven't changed! My *preferences* haven't changed. It's like... It's like lima beans. I didn't like them before my accident and I still don't like them after my accident. I tolerate them because it's rude not to when they're served as part of my family's meal, but do I suddenly like them? Have I changed my mind about loving them? *Neh*, never."

Put in those terms, Fletcher's worries about Aaron suddenly seemed absolutely ridiculous and he felt like the biggest *dummkopf* who ever lived. Yet he still couldn't quite dismiss Anna's note.

"Then how do you explain what you meant by having 'a serious concern regarding A.'?" Fletcher pressed.

Anna sat down beside him again. "Well, I could have meant any number of things," she said, counting on her fingers. "A. could stand for Amos, as in Bishop Amos. Or maybe it was short for April? Perhaps I wanted to change the date from April to March. Or possibly it stood for attendance—the list of people invited. Could I have meant arrangements? Naomi has been fretting over where the *kinner* will sleep. Perhaps I thought—"

"Okay, okay, you can stop now!" Fletcher laughed, holding up his hands. A blush crept over his face as he looked into her eyes. "I clearly let my imagination get the best of me. I don't know what to say except I'm very sorry."

Anna understood: given his history with Joyce, it wasn't any wonder he'd jumped to the wrong conclusions about the context of her note. "You're forgiven," she promised. "I'm just relieved I didn't do anything at the party to offend you."

In response, Fletcher slid his fingers between Anna's as if into a glove, sending a tingle up her arm and dispelling her concern that he wasn't a physically affectionate person.

"Somebody has been using the salve I gave him," she noticed.

"*Jah.* It's working well and it smells *gut,* too."

"You hurt yourself though," she said, indicating his thumbnail. "Poor aim?"

"Poor concentration. I was thinking about a certain *maedel.*"

"I've been thinking about you a lot, too, Fletcher. As difficult as it was, I'm glad we had this discussion."

"If the river had no rocks, it would not have a song," he quoted as he picked up a stone and tossed it into the creek.

She crumpled the note into a ball and cast it into the current, as well. "For the birds to make a nest," she said and tugged at his fingers. "Now *kumme*, let's go have dinner before my brothers eat it all."

They dropped hands before entering the kitchen, where Naomi had set a place for Fletcher.

"You're just in time for grace," she remarked warmly.

After thanking the Lord for their food and other blessings, Fletcher said to Naomi, "I hope I'm just in time to help Roy and Raymond with any house repair or yard projects you'd like finished before the wedding, too."

Anna's pulse skittered at his reference to their upcoming wedding. Although she still wasn't positive their pending nuptials would occur as scheduled, with every interaction they shared, she was growing more confident he was the husband God had provided for her.

"*Denki*, that would be appreciated," Naomi said. "There's a fence post in the yard Roy and Raymond are having trouble setting and I'd like your opinion on the window in the attic. It feels drafty up there and I don't want our guests' *kinner* to catch a chill."

"I noticed a loose floorboard in the mudroom, too," Fletcher commented. "The boys and I may also have to take a look at the porch stairs."

The three young men clomped into the mudroom. Eli and Evan were tasked with helping Naomi till the soil for her gardens while Anna focused on scrubbing the floors. In deference to Dr. Donovan's advice, she stopped short of beating the rugs herself, instead hanging them so Melinda could complete the task later that afternoon. The day took on a festive air and by the time the group stopped for supper, they'd accomplished more than they'd set out to.

"If it's alright with you, Anna, I'd like to take you for a ride after supper," Fletcher said over dessert.

"Not so fast." Naomi waved a finger at him, "You still need to address the draft in the attic."

"Of course," Fletcher agreed. "I meant after that."

"Why the disappointed expression? You're being let off easy," his future mother-in-law teased. She turned to her sons. "When your *daed* was keen on me, he volunteered to help your *groossdaadi* build an entire house just for the chance to say hello to me when I came out with a pitcher of water."

Anna fidgeted in her chair and glanced at Fletcher, who was studiously focused on scraping the ice cream from his bowl. Nothing escaped Naomi's notice.

"There's no need to be embarrassed, you two. It would serve most couples well to remember after they're married how eager they were to spend time in each other's company before they wed." Naomi sighed, wiping the corner of her eye. "Time spent with those we love is one of *Gott*'s most precious gifts. We ought to value it more dearly because it passes so quickly."

"Mamm," Evan whined, "the last time Melinda and Aaron mentioned mushy grown-up love talk at the table, you said my ears were too young to hear that kind of thing."

The others joined Naomi in laughter. "That's right," she said, patting his head. "How about if we talk about turtles instead?"

By the time Anna finished washing and putting away the dishes and Fletcher and the boys installed insulation and repaired the window in the attic, it was dusk.

"Why don't we have a cup of tea on the porch instead of going for a ride?" Anna suggested.

They sat side by side on the swing, gently swaying as they chatted. The rhythmic motion lulled Anna into a deep sense of relaxation, and she rested her head against Fletcher's shoulder. Lowering her lids, she imagined the two of them spending evenings like this on the porch of their own house. She could picture their children romping on the front lawn and in her imagination they all had Fletcher's lustrous wavy hair and intense blue eyes.

"Are you tired?" he asked.

"*Neh*, I'm peaceful," she replied. "In fact, I haven't felt this peaceful in a long time."

"That's too bad," Fletcher said. "Because there's something I want to show you, but you'll have to get up and *kumme* with me."

He took her by the hand, caressing her icy fingers to warm them as they made their way to the expansive maple in the backyard. Its branches appeared black against the ebbing light of the sky, which was beginning to glisten with early stars.

Anna tittered when they stopped beneath its mighty boughs. "Did we argue under this tree, too, as we did when we first met beneath the willow?"

"Hardly," Fletcher replied and his voice sounded gravelly. "You really don't remember what happened here?"

Noticing his impassioned tone, she paused, wishing she could claim every second of their courtship was etched indelibly across her heart. "I'm sorry, Fletcher," she admitted, "but I don't."

Fletcher reached for Anna's shoulders, gently positioning her against the trunk. "Well, you were standing like this. And I was leaning with my hand here, above you. Your hair was dappled with bits of light and your eyes mirrored the greenery all around us."

Fletcher gently touched Anna's cheek with the back of his hand, remembering.

"What happened next?" she whispered.

"May I show you?"

"You may."

He leaned toward her for a soft kiss.

After a quiet pause, he had to know if she experienced the same depth of emotion he felt. "Now do you remember?" he asked.

"I may not remember the first time," Anna spoke slowly, "but I won't forget this time."

Fletcher's heart pranced. It wasn't exactly the answer he'd hoped to hear, but it was the next best thing.

"Evan would be disappointed to hear you couldn't remember the first time," he joked, leading her back toward the house.

"Evan?"

"*Jah.* You and I were sharing our first kiss when you were supposed to be watching Timothy the Turtle. That's how he wandered away."

Anna's laughter rang out through the darkness. "That's terrible!"

Terrible for Timothy, but wunderbaar *for me*, Fletcher thought as he ambled up the steps to accompany Anna to the door. "I suppose it's time to say *gut nacht.*"

"Could you please help me find the teacups,

first?" Anna requested. "It's gotten dark and I'm not sure I'll be able to see where we set them."

As they cautiously advanced toward the front of the porch, Fletcher abruptly stopped, realizing there was someone sitting in the swing.

"I don't know what Naomi's so upset about," Melinda was saying. "I was only an hour or two late. She's such a worrywart. Besides, if we had arrived in time for supper, she wouldn't have asked you to stay, even though Fletcher was invited."

Fletcher coughed to signal Melinda he could hear her, while from behind, Anna loudly cut her short with, "Is that you, Melinda?"

"*Jah*, and I'm with her," Aaron answered. "Where did the two of you *kumme* from?"

"We were taking a stroll. Enjoying the evening air," Anna responded curtly as she and Fletcher approached the other couple. They were still holding hands and if Fletcher wasn't mistaken, Anna tightened her grasp as she spoke.

"See what I mean?" Melinda continued, unabashed to have been caught complaining about them. "Naomi gives you and Fletcher her blessing to do whatever you want whenever you want. It's not fair."

"*Neh*, what's not fair, Melinda," Anna rebutted, "is that everyone in this household, including Fletcher, has been working all afternoon on house and yard projects that need to be completed before the weddings. Yet you didn't arrive home until after seven o'clock, even though your shift at Schrock's ended at four. If you want Aaron to be included at mealtime, the two of you ought to consider pitching in."

Melinda shifted in her seat and began to protest, but Anna wasn't finished speaking.

"As for Naomi being a worrywart, it's true," she said. "Naomi often frets when the people she *cares* about aren't home when they should be. In part that's because the last time someone other than you didn't return home on time was when I had my accident, and the time before that was when my *daed* died. So you—and Aaron— should think about what goes through Naomi's mind when you decide to amble home several hours after you're expected!"

Anna dropped Fletcher's hand as she stooped to pick up a teacup and saucer near the side of the swing. Fletcher retrieved the other cup and saucer from where Anna left it balanced on the railing and wordlessly followed her to the side door. When she turned to say good-night, Anna's hand was shaking so furiously that the cup rattled against the saucer. Fletcher took the china from her and stacked it with his on the bench beside them. He gingerly ran a finger beneath her chin, tilting her face upward. It was too dark to read the expression in her eyes, but he felt the wetness of a tear moisten his skin.

"Anna," he whispered. "This evening has been too special to allow anything to spoil it."

"I know it has and it still is." She sniffed. "But there are still many memories about our courtship I hope will return to me, so I don't want Melinda's rude comments about your presence here to keep you from visiting me as often as possible in the next two and a half weeks before the wedding."

"Are you joking? Wild horses couldn't keep me away!"

"Do you promise?" Anna asked.

"I promise and I'll even seal it with a kiss," Fletcher pledged, bending to brush his lips against hers.

On the way home, he marveled over the amount of time he'd spent anguishing over Anna's note, when he could have spoken to her about it earlier and alleviated his fears. Even if she still couldn't say for certain what she meant by her message, her guesses seemed more likely than the assumption he'd made. He belatedly reckoned his experience with Joyce had colored his perception, but he wasn't going to allow it to cast a shadow on his relationship with Anna any longer. No, after their conversation—and their kisses—this evening, Fletcher was thoroughly convinced she carried a torch for him and him alone.

"*Denki*, Lord!" he prayed aloud as his horse trotted through the night. "*Denki* for Your grace and goodness toward Anna and me, by providing us for each other and by keeping my foolishness from destroying our relationship."

In light of his conversation with Anna, any misgivings he'd felt toward his cousin dissolved completely and soon he was asking God to bless Aaron's marriage to Melinda, too. *The two of them seem to need all the prayer and help they can get before becoming husband and wife*, he mused.

But by the time Fletcher stretched out on his bed, Melinda and Aaron were far from his mind. His only thoughts were of Anna: Anna beneath the willow and Anna under the maple; Anna in sunlight and Anna in starlight; Anna then and Anna now. *Anna, Anna, Anna*, he mumbled drowsily before dozing off. *My bride-to-be.*

Chapter Eight

On Sunday morning, Anna sat bolt upright in bed, unsure whether the vision that just raced through her mind was a memory or a dream. In it, Fletcher had just kissed her and she was filled with repulsion. The images were fuzzy, but the way they made her feel was undeniably clear and Anna shuddered violently.

"What's wrong with you?" Melinda muttered, squinting one eye at her.

"I had a nightmare, that's all," Anna replied.

Melinda rolled over and pulled the quilt up to her ears, but Anna got up, made her bed and dressed and then padded downstairs to begin making breakfast before the family held their home church services. She was cubing potatoes for breakfast when the image of kissing Fletcher crossed her mind again, except this time she recalled his hands gripping her shoulders as well as the breeze lifting his dark, wavy hair when he pulled her toward him for an emphatic kiss.

Disconcerted that the dream played itself out in her waking moments, Anna sat down at the table and covered her eyes with her hand. *I must be overly tired*, she thought. *My mind is playing tricks on me.*

"Are you okay?" Eli cheeped, startling her.

She jumped up and said, "*Guder mariye*, Eli. *Jah*, I'm fine. I was just resting my eyes before I started making breakfast casserole. Look, I'm going to use bacon instead of sausage, the way you like it. I notice you haven't been eating a lot lately."

The boy's eyes brightened. "*Denki*, Anna. I'll go get the eggs from the henhouse."

Naomi was the next person awake. "That smells *gut* already, Anna. But you should allow me to make breakfast. I'll have to get used to cooking all our meals again once you move out."

"Mmm," Anna said noncommittally.

Naomi immediately panicked. "Uh-oh. Is something wrong? Did you and Fletcher decide not to carry through with your wedding? You were getting on so well yesterday."

Anna chuckled. "All I said was 'mmm.'"

"*Jah*, but it was the way you said it," insisted Naomi.

Eli burst into the kitchen with his basket

of eggs. *"Guder mariye, Mamm,"* he greeted Naomi. "Anna's putting bacon in the casserole instead of sausage."

"Just the way somebody in this family likes it, but I can't remember who," Naomi teased.

"Me!" Eli cheered.

"I guess your sister has a better memory than I do," Naomi said. "She must have decided to make it specially tailored for you, because you're the first one up. Now please go wake everyone else—without shouting."

After Eli dashed out of the room, Anna replied to her stepmother's earlier question. "Nothing went wrong between Fletcher and me. In fact, yesterday was one of the best days we've had together yet."

"But?" Naomi asked, setting the plates around the table.

Anna sighed; Naomi was so perceptive. "But I guess I'd still like to remember more about our courtship and I'd still like to find my journal," she admitted. "I think that would allay any lingering qualms I might have."

Especially after this morning's nightmare, she thought.

"I can't make your memories return, although I'll continue to pray about that," Naomi offered. "As for your journal, we've practically turned the house inside out with our spring cleaning, so it seems we would have found it by now. Is it possible you stashed it in the stable?"

"I doubt it," Anna said, "although it's worth a look."

"Guder mariye," Roy, Raymond and Evan greeted the women before taking their seats.

"I couldn't get Melinda to wake up," Eli reported, wiggling onto a chair.

"She's probably tired because she was out on the porch late last night with Aaron," Evan commented knowingly.

"Evan, what did *Mamm* tell us about eavesdropping?" Eli chastised his younger brother.

"I wasn't eavesdropping," he insisted innocently. "The window was stuck open."

"Oh! I'm sorry," Anna quickly apologized. "I couldn't get it down again after I washed it. I hope you boys weren't too cold last night. Roy or Raymond, you should take a look at how it sits in the frame."

"See? That wasn't my fault so it doesn't count as eavesdropping," Evan retorted to Eli. "Besides, I didn't even repeat that I heard Melinda asking Aaron if he was jellies because Fletcher is marrying Anna, not him. And Aaron said if he was jellies, would he do this, then she said to stop that because it tickles and then she kept laughing."

"Melinda didn't ask Aaron if he was jellies,

Evan," Eli hotly refuted. "She asked him if he was *jealous*, but you still repeated gossip because you just told everyone."

"Boys!" Naomi squawked, clapping her hands sharply together once. That's all the reprimand they needed to stop talking.

No one else said a word, either, until Melinda sidled into the room. "It's so quiet in here, I thought maybe it wasn't an off-Sunday and you'd all left for church without me," she joked as she heaped casserole onto her plate.

After everyone had eaten their fill, Anna cleared the table, contemplating Evan's disclosure about the conversation he'd overheard. She knew Melinda had come up with some ludicrous theories in her time, but this one took the cake. If Aaron was envious of Fletcher, it was because of Fletcher's inherent character and his superior abilities—it had nothing to do with Fletcher marrying Anna. Still, Anna hoped Melinda and Aaron had resolved the issue; the last thing she wanted was more tension between her and her cousin. Anna felt bad enough about her strong words from the previous night as it was.

Once they finished worshipping together, Evan asked if Anna would accompany him and Eli to the stream.

"Why not?" she asked, eager to lighten the mood after their morning squabble.

"Watch yourselves around the rocks," Naomi cautioned, waving goodbye.

The trio spritely marched through the dewy grass, down the hill and across the meadow. Once they arrived at the creek, Anna alighted on the boulder nearest the willow. Due to the spring rains, the creek's current was moving swiftly and she kept a close eye on the boys as they attempted to chuck stones across to the opposite bank. She was thinking about how the willow's lengthy fringe dancing in the breeze reminded her of a woman's long hair, when she was struck with another memory like the one that had afflicted her earlier that morning.

In the recollection, Fletcher stood not five feet from where Evan was now pitching a rock into the rushing water. He had just kissed her and she was trying to secure her prayer *kapp* over her hair, which had become mussed when she jerked away from him. She recalled that they had argued and she was crying. As the scant details manifested in her mind's eye, Anna's knees trembled and she began to pant, trying to catch her breath.

"Boys," she weakly summoned them. "It's time to go. *Kumme*, take my hands, please. I'm not feeling quite right."

They steadied her up the hill and delivered her into Naomi's care.

"You're as pale as a sheet and shaking like a leaf," Naomi fretted. "I never should have permitted you to do so much last week. I'm sending Raymond to the phone shanty to call Dr. Donovan."

"*Neh*, please don't," Anna argued feebly as her teeth chattered. "I j-just need to get warm. It was nippy near the creek. Dr. Donovan's office is probably closed for the weekend anyway."

Naomi scrutinized Anna's face. Finally, she allowed, "I'll put on a pot of tea and Melinda will draw you a bath. We'll see how you're doing after that. But if I suspect so much as a hint of a fever, I'll have Raymond bring us to the hospital straightaway."

Although she couldn't stomach the tea and toast Naomi prepared for her, Anna stopped shaking after taking a bath. At her stepmother's insistence, she nestled into Naomi's bed, where Naomi swaddled her in quilts and set a bell at her side to ring if she needed assistance. But Anna only wanted to be alone, and once she was, she wept into her arms, wishing she could forget the very memories she'd been praying so fervently to recall.

When Fletcher arrived at Anna's house on Sunday afternoon, Naomi greeted him at the door. Her skin was wan and her eyes were bloodshot. "*Guder nammidaag*, Fletcher. I'm afraid I can't invite you in. Anna has taken ill and Eli is sick, too. I don't want you to catch whatever is plaguing our household."

Fletcher's heart raced. Anna was ill? But at least it couldn't have been related to her concussion, since Eli was also sick, right? "Is there something I can do to help?" he asked.

"*Neh.* Neither one of them has a fever. And although Eli's had terrible stomach pains, they seem to have subsided. Right now I think rest is the best thing for both of them."

"May I call on Anna this evening?" Fletcher asked.

"*Neh,*" Naomi responded sharply before softening her tone. "I'm sorry, Fletcher, but I fear it was my fault she overdid it last week, which is why she's sick now, so I have to put my foot down. I'll be sure to tell her you asked after her and wanted to see her, but I wouldn't allow it."

"But—"

"If you don't want her to risk having to return to the hospital, you'll support her recovery by allowing her to rest," Naomi reiterated firmly.

Fletcher couldn't argue with Naomi's logic, so he reluctantly returned home. Once there, he found himself at a loss for things to do. He'd already spent the morning in worship with his uncle's family, and usually Anna and her brothers were the only people he visited during off-Sundays. Since moving to Willow Creek, he'd been befriended by a few of the older men in the district, but he didn't feel comfortable dropping in on them and their families uninvited.

Since it was the Sabbath, all but the most essential work was prohibited. As it was, he'd already completed everything except painting the alcove he'd created for Anna, and he routinely kept up the stable and yard. In regard to the house's interior, it was tidy, but he realized it definitely needed a woman's touch. *Soon enough*, he thought as he sat down in the parlor.

He read Scripture for an hour and then enjoyed a long nap. When he awoke, he decided to write his sisters, as he was long overdue in replying to their letter.

Dear Esther, Leah, Rebekah & Families,
I hope this note finds everyone healthy. Thank you for your good wishes and faithful prayers, as expressed in your last letter. I am sorry for my delay in responding. I'm afraid I've been distracted because Anna recently suffered a head injury that resulted in substantial memory loss. Rest assured, she is recovering well. Physically, she no longer suffers from the headaches or nausea she endured immediately following her

fall, and her recollections are also returning to her. Still, I covet your prayers for her complete healing.

I look forward to hearing all about what has been happening in your lives when we talk in person at the wedding, if not by letter before then.

Until then, may the Lord bless you.
—Fletcher.

After he affixed a stamp to the envelope, Fletcher carried the letter to the mailbox for the carrier to pick up the following day. When he unlatched the door to the box, a flurry of envelopes fluttered to the ground and he snorted to realize it must have been days since he'd retrieved the mail; clearly he valued the notes Raymond delivered much more than those the carrier brought. Most of the spilled items were advertisements and bills, but one was a personal letter written in a hand he didn't immediately recognize. Tearing it open as he walked, he read:

Fletcher,
I've heard the news that you are soon to be wed and I hope you will accept my sincere congratulations. I also hope you will permit me this belated apology for the anguish I caused. Whether you believe me or

not, I didn't deliberately intend to deceive you. I honestly didn't know my own heart. That is, I honestly didn't fully comprehend how I felt about Frederick until it was almost too late.

For both of our sakes, I'm grateful you and I didn't marry and I trust you are even more grateful than I. In any case, I pray for you all of the love and happiness you so richly deserve. May the Lord bless your marriage abundantly.
Joyce Wittmer.

Fletcher stopped in his tracks and reread the note. On one hand, he was appalled that Joyce had the nerve to write him—especially because she said how grateful she was they hadn't gotten married! On the other hand, she was right: he was even more grateful than she was. If it hadn't been for Joyce calling off their wedding, Fletcher never would have discovered what true love was, because he wouldn't have moved to Willow Creek and met Anna. As for forgiving Joyce, he'd done that long ago, even if he occasionally battled leftover feelings related to their breakup. But Fletcher accepted her apology for what it was: an earnest expression of contrition.

When he got inside, he crumpled up the note and threw it in the woodstove. It was a reminder of old hurts that belonged to the past. He was looking ahead now, to his future with Anna. As he stirred a pot of canned soup for supper, he thought about the tender kisses they'd shared the day before, and he imagined those they'd exchange in the future; perhaps even as soon as tomorrow. He ate quickly and, despite having taken a nap, he turned in to bed early, hoping to hasten the arrival of a new day.

Instead, he slept fitfully and the night seemed to stretch on twice as long as usual. As he listlessly twisted this way and that, a single unbidden thought came to mind: *What if Anna doesn't know her own heart, either?* He dismissed the idea almost the second he thought it, chalking it up to his thwarted longing to see her again. But his restlessness kept him awake for hours, until he finally decided to dress and go to work, arriving well before the break of dawn.

He was surprised when Roy and Raymond walked in carrying a battery-powered nail gun and drill less than a half an hour after sunrise.

"Guder mariye," Fletcher said. He barely waited for a reply before asking, "How's Anna?"

"I think she's alright," Roy replied. *"Mamm* took her some broth last night and she finished it all."

"But there's no note for you," Raymond said,

anticipating Fletcher's question. "She was still sleeping when we left."

Although his hope was deflated, Fletcher responded, "That's okay. I'm sure I'll speak to her tonight. Do you two need a hand carrying in more tools?"

"*Neh*, there's only one more load. We've got it," Raymond replied as the brothers exited and Aaron entered.

He looked startled to see Fletcher. "What time did you get here?"

"An hour and a half ago," Fletcher replied.

"Why are you always doing that?" Aaron challenged him, setting down the portable table saw with a loud clatter.

"Doing what?" Fletcher had no idea what the problem was.

"You've always got to show me up. Staying later, coming in earlier. What are you trying to prove?"

"Aaron, I'm *helping* you, not *competing* with you," Fletcher argued.

"Well, don't think just because you came in early you're going to leave early. The entire reason I'm here now is because we've got to finish up this floor today. I took another contract that starts tomorrow morning."

Fletcher resisted the urge to ask Aaron why he accepted another simultaneous project when they clearly weren't finished with this one. He could tell his cousin was tense enough as it was, so instead, Fletcher channeled his frustration into performing his work, motivating himself with the fact that the sooner they finished, the sooner he'd get to see Anna again.

On Monday, Anna lingered in bed. After Sunday's long nap and a good night's rest, her quivering had stopped, but she kept her eyes closed, trying to convince herself that yesterday's recurrent unpleasant memory of kissing Fletcher was only a dream. Yet deep down she knew sooner or later, she'd have to ask for Fletcher's help in making sense of the awful image that kept coming to mind. He'd told her he didn't want her to hide anything from him, didn't he? But what would she say? How could she tell him, "I have a vague recollection of kissing you at the creek and being wholly repulsed"? After his vulnerable confession the other day, she didn't want to shake his confidence about her feelings for him.

"Are you still asleep or are you just pretending so you won't have to make breakfast?" Melinda whispered.

"Neither," Anna said, raising her lids. "I'm awake but I'm not deliberately trying to get out of helping with breakfast. That would be irresponsible."

"Oh," Melinda said, seemingly deaf to Anna's

reproach. "I was wondering, how far have you progressed with your wedding dress?"

"I've got considerable work to do," Anna responded vaguely, sitting up. Although she was certain she hadn't moved her wedding dress fabric from the other side of the attic, it was no longer there. For fear of being teased about her forgetfulness by her cousin, Anna didn't want to inquire if Melinda had moved it. "Why do you ask?"

"Well, since Naomi will likely confine you to our room today anyway, do you suppose you'd mind making some adjustments to the sleeves and hem on mine? Joseph has asked me to work extra hours at the shop and I don't see how I'll finish my dress unless you help me."

Anna felt like suggesting Melinda might try staying in instead of running around with Aaron every night. But since she knew her suggestion was futile, she reluctantly agreed. "Alright, try it on and let me see what needs to be done."

As her cousin was changing into the violet dress and she was making her bed, Anna asked, "So, Joseph wants you to work extra hours at the shop?"

"*Jah*, he even mentioned keeping me on after you return. Sales are up since I started working there," Melinda boasted as she climbed onto a stool so Anna could examine the hem.

Anna held pins pressed between her lips and she didn't reply.

"I think it's because I have a way with *Englisch* customers," Melinda babbled. "Tessa Fisher barely utters two words to them, so I think they appreciate having a chatty, comely Amish girl like me to approach— Ouch! You pricked me with that pin!"

"Did I?" Anna asked innocently. "Turn toward me, please."

"How do I look?" Melinda hinted.

"Crooked." Anna frowned, smoothing the hem.

"Not the dress—*me*," Melinda emphasized.

Anna took a step backward and tipped her head upward for a better look at the full dress. The color accentuated Melinda's dark hair and eyes, gathering modestly over the curves of her girlish figure. She would make a beautiful bride.

Anna answered honestly, "You look lovely, absolutely lovely." Which was exactly how Anna wanted to feel in her own wedding dress.

It's not fair, she thought in an instant of self-pity. *Why should Melinda get to experience such excitement about her wedding, when I've experienced little but anxiety about mine?*

"Denki," Melinda said, hopping down from the stool and twirling in a circle before giving Anna a hug. *"Denki* for everything, Anna. If it

weren't for you, I wouldn't be getting married and I wouldn't have a job at the shop. In a way, it's almost a blessing you had a concussion."

Annoyed by Melinda's complete lack of sensitivity, Anna tugged her cousin's arms from around her neck. "Stop that," she snapped. "You're hurting me." *And I've been in pain for long enough as it is.*

After dressing, she made her way into the kitchen where she said good morning to Naomi and then asked, "Are Raymond and Roy out milking?"

"*Neh*, Aaron picked the boys up very early this morning. How do you feel today?"

"As strong as an ox," Anna claimed. She supposed it was just as well the boys had left before she could send a note with Raymond, since she wasn't sure what to write to Fletcher anyway. She figured he'd come for supper and by then she would have collected her thoughts.

"Oh, am I ever relieved to hear that!" Naomi exclaimed. Then she said, "This morning, I'll be taking Evan to school and dropping Melinda off in town, and then I'm stopping at the phone shanty to make an appointment for Eli at the clinic in Highland Springs."

"The clinic in Highland Springs?" Anna repeated. The *Englisch*-run clinic offered pediatric care exclusively to members of the Amish community. "What's wrong with Eli?"

"He was sick to his stomach shortly after you returned from the creek. His cramps came and went all night, but he doesn't have a fever. I recall his stomach hurting him the other day, too, so I want to be sure there's nothing seriously wrong."

"That's a *gut* idea," Anna agreed. "I'll stay here with him now and then accompany you to his appointment when you get back."

As it turned out, Naomi couldn't schedule an appointment until four o'clock. She sat next to Anna in the front seat, while Eli curled up with a hot water bottle in the back. Once they arrived at the clinic, Naomi was softly reading aloud to her son when the disturbing image again troubled Anna's mind.

"I'm going to stretch my legs," she announced before ambling down the long corridor.

She was examining a colorful mural of barnyard animals when a voice behind her resounded, "Anna! What brings you to the children's clinic?"

She recognized his voice before she angled around to greet him. "Hello, Dr. Donovan." She couldn't help but smile when speaking to the kind man. "My brother has a stomachache."

"Ah, we get a lot of those around here. I mean,

our patients do. I volunteer here once a month," he explained. "Usually, the stomachaches are nothing serious. But what about you, how are you feeling?"

"I'm fine," Anna said, but to her dismay, her eyes unexpectedly spouted fat tears.

Dr. Donovan clasped her elbow, ushering her into an empty office, where he motioned for her to sit. Then he passed a box of tissues across the desk and clasped his hands over his belly while she blew her nose. "I take it your memories haven't returned then, eh?" he asked.

"Actually, they have. Not too many of Fletcher or our courtship, but plenty of other people and events."

"That's a good sign, yet you're not happy?"

"I'm... I'm frustrated. And confused," she confessed. "At first, my recollection of the past six months seemed as blank as a field of snow. Now when the memories come back, some of them remind me of scuffling along a winding path covered with fallen leaves. They're turned every which way and I can't make sense of them. I don't know what's a memory and what's a dream."

Dr. Donovan bobbed his head vigorously. "Those are excellent metaphors for what it feels like to have your memories return. I've never heard a patient describe the process quite like that, but it's very common for them to tell me their recollections are fuzzy, foggy or dream-like."

"It's common?" Anna raised her eyebrows. "Then how do your patients know what really happened and what didn't?"

"As I've said before, it takes time for the brain to heal. I'd suggest you hold on to your recollections loosely for the time being, because things aren't always as they seem to be. Meanwhile, trust this," Dr. Donovan advised, placing his hand over his heart. "Not this," he added, pointing to his head.

Her mind eased, Anna gushed, "Thank you, Dr. Donovan! Thank you!" as his phone buzzed.

She closed the door behind her and stepped into the hall to find Naomi approaching. Eli was holding her hand and sucking on a lollipop. It occurred to Anna he looked healthier and more energetic than his *mamm* did. After Naomi confirmed the doctor said there was nothing wrong with Eli that two more days of a restricted diet wouldn't cure, they walked to the buggy.

By the time Anna steered them through an especially grueling rush hour traffic jam and up the lane to their house, it was six o'clock. Naomi said she had a blinding headache, so Anna advised her to lie down, even though by then her own head was beginning to pound. Figuring she was probably only peckish, Anna anticipated a good hot meal would revive her and she swiftly stabled the horse before entering the house, where it was clear Melinda hadn't started supper. When she found her cousin in the sitting room with her *kapp* askew and her arms draped around Aaron's neck, Anna clenched her teeth. Couldn't Melinda ever be counted on to perform the most basic tasks without being prompted? Anna's knees felt wobbly and she steadied herself against the doorframe.

"Are you alright, Anna?" Aaron asked and his voice was so sympathetic, for a moment he sounded just like Fletcher. But then he added, "You look as if you've been wrestling a greased pig."

"And she lost," Melinda added, crowing uproariously.

"I'm fine, *denki* for asking," Anna replied in her politest voice to show they hadn't ruffled her feathers. But suddenly, she changed her mind and said. "Actually, Melinda, *you're* the one who looks as if she's been wrestling a greased pig—and he's sitting right there beside you!"

Then she spun around, leaving them to stare at each other in shocked silence.

Fletcher was exhausted. It was nine o'clock and he wasn't nearly finished laying the customer's floor. As he headed for home, he mentally reviewed the dispute he'd had with Aaron earlier that afternoon.

"You know what Anna said about how worried their *mamm* gets when they arrive home later than expected," Aaron argued after announcing he was leaving work at four o'clock and taking Roy and Raymond with him.

"*Jah*, but I can't finish this project on my own. Why don't you just take Roy and leave Raymond here with me? I'll bring him home when we've finished."

"*Jah,*" Raymond said. "I'll stay here."

"I can stay, too," Roy volunteered. "I need to learn all the steps of installing flooring. Since you said you arranged to pick up Melinda in town anyway, you can just ask her to relay the message to *Mamm* that we'll be late."

"See what you've done?" Aaron asked Fletcher. "You've trained the apprentice to think his preferences override the foreman's decision."

Fletcher saw the sense in what Raymond and Roy were suggesting and he appreciated their dedication. But, from his recent heated interaction with Aaron, he also recognized his cousin probably felt his authority was being challenged, so Fletcher tried to show his support.

"They respect the fact that you're in charge," he said. "They were only trying to be helpful."

"If they want to be helpful, fine, they can be helpful, but it will have to be on a volunteer basis. They've been here for over eight hours already today and we've got a busy week in front of us. I can't pay them to stay after hours."

Fletcher again tried to reason with his cousin. "Look at that section there—it hasn't even been stapled yet. Then we've got to take care of the baseboards, the gaps, the puttying—"

"I know the order of layering a floor," Aaron jeered. "Listen, we tried our best to finish it today, but it just wasn't possible. If you feel obligated to keep working on it, that's up to you, but I've made my plans for the evening clear and I'm not changing them."

Fletcher was so frustrated he couldn't speak. He couldn't understand why Aaron didn't pride himself on his work ethic, the way virtually all Amish people did. Yet even as the thought entered his mind, he realized he was guilty of judging another person. Running his hand over his face, he silently prayed, *Dear* Gott, *please forgive me for judging my cousin and enable me to be a help, not a hindrance, to my* onkel*'s business.*

"Fletcher," Raymond suggested, "maybe you should take a break. *Kumme* have supper with us and then we'll all return to put in a few more hours—how's that?"

"Speak for yourself!" Aaron chortled.

"*Neh*, you go ahead," Fletcher told Raymond. "But let me give you a note for Anna."

After finding a scrap of paper, he removed the pencil he kept tucked behind his ear. *Dear Anna*, he wrote. *I hope you are feeling better. I have to work late tonight, but I will see you to-morrow. I haven't forgotten my promise.*

While he paused, deliberating whether to sign the note "your Fletcher," or just plain "Fletcher," Aaron ribbed him, "Hurry up, will you? I'm hungry!" So he simply signed the note "F."

Now, some five hours later, Fletcher decided he'd better let Aaron know he was unable to complete the project and they'd need to return in the early morning. He made a detour toward his uncle's house. There was still a lamp lit in the kitchen, so he gave a quick rap on the door before entering the house, where he found Isaiah sitting at the table, drinking something that appeared to be lemonade.

"It's apple cider vinegar, lemon juice, ginger, honey and everything else except the kitchen sink," his uncle joked, raising the mason jar. "It's supposed to help my arthritis. Want some?"

Fletcher laughed. "*Denki*, but I'll pass. I stopped by to talk to Aaron. Is he still up?"

"Up? He's not home yet," Isaiah said. "I'm

waiting for him myself. Is there a message you want me to pass along to him?"

"Well…" Fletcher hesitated. He was concerned he might get Aaron in trouble with his father if Isaiah found out they hadn't completed a project before taking on a new one again.

Isaiah prompted him, "At this time of night, there must be a *gut* reason you came here."

"*Jah*, if you could tell him I'll be installing the floor early tomorrow morning, I'd appreciate it."

"Will do," Isaiah confirmed.

Fletcher was about to board his buggy when he heard the familiar plodding of a horse's hooves, so he waited until his cousin pulled into the yard and explained the situation to him.

Uncharacteristically amenable, Aaron said, "That's fine. I'll join you, if I can pull myself from bed that early. I didn't mean to stay out so late, but you know how it is when you're having fun—you lose track of time. You should have been there. After Anna made supper, we all played Dutch Blitz for hours."

"Anna doesn't like to play Dutch Blitz," Fletcher argued. "She says it makes her head swim."

"That goes to show how well you really know your fiancée," Aaron responded. "She not only suggested the game, she beat us all!"

How could that be? Fletcher wondered, long

into the night. *She told me her preferences hadn't changed.* His old worry about what else she might feel differently about plagued his thoughts almost until the sun came up, and by then it was time for him to rise, too.

Chapter Nine

The next morning Anna got up early to fix a tray of coffee, eggs and toast for Naomi before making breakfast for the rest of the family.

"Are you awake, Naomi?" she asked as she slowly pushed open the door to her stepmother's room.

"Oh, *guder mariye*, Anna," Naomi replied, lifting her head from the pillow. "This looks *wunderbaar*, but I feel much better now. I can get up."

"Please don't," Anna pleaded. "I've already checked on Eli and he's sleeping peacefully, so I thought I'd sit here with you and drink my *kaffi* before the boys *kumme* in from milking. I stayed up too late last night."

Naomi held a forkful of eggs midair. "You weren't ill again, were you?"

"*Neh*, I played several games of Dutch Blitz

with Melinda, Aaron and the boys. It was nearly nine o'clock when we stopped and then I had to do the dishes."

"But I thought you loathe playing Dutch Blitz?"

"I do…but I was trying to make peace with Melinda and Aaron. Lately I've made a few comments to them I wish I hadn't."

"Whatever you said, I have a hunch they deserved it."

"You wouldn't be saying that if you'd heard the remark I made to them yesterday," Anna hinted before detailing her exchange with them.

"Oh dear," was all Naomi said when Anna was finished.

"I told you it was bad!" Anna lamented. "What I need to do is apologize. Do you suppose I could make a special dinner tonight and invite Aaron, by way of smoothing things over?"

"But you've been ill—"

"I'm all better now," Anna asserted. "In fact, at the clinic yesterday I bumped into Dr. Donovan and we discussed what was ailing me and he said everything I'm experiencing is perfectly normal." Anna didn't clarify that what was ailing her was emotional, not physical.

"Really?" Naomi questioned. "I'm so glad to hear it! In that case, *jah*, we can serve a special dinner tonight. I was invited to Ruth Graber's for supper this evening, but I'll stay home to help you instead—"

"Neh!" Anna butted in. "You deserve a night out with your friends. Please go!"

Naomi hesitated before surrendering. "I'll go under one condition," she stated seriously, holding up her finger for effect. "Whatever you do, don't make ham or pork chops for dinner. Otherwise, Melinda and Aaron might question how sincere you are about apologizing for calling anyone's behavior piggish!"

They burst into laughter as the door swung open. It was Eli, declaring he was starving. While Naomi went to fix breakfast, Anna returned to her room to tell Melinda about the special supper, but her cousin had a pillow covering her head and was snoring softly.

Anna took out a notepad and wrote, *Dear Fletcher, I hope you will be able to come to supper tonight.* Without thinking twice, she signed it, *Your Anna.* Then, she scribbled an invitation to Aaron, too. *Aaron, you're invited to join us for supper tonight. —Anna.*

For their meal, Anna made beef stew and corn bread, with sugar cream pie for dessert, since it was Melinda's and Aaron's favorite treat. After Naomi had left for the evening and the four boys were finishing their evening chores in the stable,

Anna approached Melinda and Aaron in the sitting room to apologize before Fletcher arrived.

"I want to apologize to you both for the remark I made the other day," she said, glad the room was dim so they couldn't see the heat rising in her cheeks. "I hope you'll forgive me."

Melinda stuck out her lower lip. "If you must know, I've grown accustomed to your surly disposition since the accident and I've learned to overlook it, but Aaron isn't used to your attitude. He was upset for a long part of the evening, weren't you, Aaron?"

Anna linked her fingers behind her back, squeezing them together as tightly as she could as a reminder to hold her tongue, even though she was thinking that Aaron wasn't so upset he couldn't play several games of cards.

"Jah," he admitted. "I never expected you to make such a churlish remark, Anna."

Please, Lord, she silently prayed, *give me grace*. "I understand how surprising that must have been for you," was as close as she could come to expressing further regret. "I assure you it won't happen again. Now *kumme*, supper is ready."

"Wait!" Aaron leaped to his feet, positioning himself directly in front of Anna and boring into her eyes with his. "I'm sorry, too. I could sense you were in pain or upset and I... I tried joking to make you laugh. I always used to be able to make you feel better, but lately, it's as if... I don't know, as if we're enemies or something."

Anna's feet seemed nailed to the floor and her mouth fell open. She hadn't heard Aaron sound so contrite since before Melinda came to live there. Perhaps she'd been judging him too harshly?

"We're not enemies at all," she said, smiling graciously to prove her point. "In fact, we're about to become family."

"Now there's the dimple I've missed seeing!" Aaron declared, taking a step closer.

"Am I too late?" Fletcher asked from behind Anna.

She twirled, eager to see his toothy grin once more, but she was met with a somber frown. *"Neh,"* she consoled him. "That's the *gut* thing about stew. It can simmer on the stove until we're ready to eat it, which we are! *Kumme.*"

"Stew?" Aaron sounded pleased. "Did you make corn bread, too?"

"Jah," Anna replied distractedly, leading them to the table.

"I haven't had your stew and corn bread for ages," he commented. "No one makes it quite the way you do."

During their meal, Eli and Evan recounted the fiasco they'd witnessed that day in school when one of the oldest scholars got wedged between the rungs of the porch stairs during lunch hour and couldn't get free. Then, the men summarized their newest project at work, and afterward, Melinda described her activities assisting customers at the shop.

"It's always so busy there," she remarked to Anna. "I enjoy it, but sometimes I long for the days when I was home and I could have a cup of tea or take a little nap whenever I wanted."

"I'm sure you do," Anna replied, getting up to bring the pie to the table.

"Is that sugar cream pie?" Aaron asked. "My favorite!"

"It's one of Melinda's favorites, too," Anna said. "That's why I made it."

"Will we need forks to eat it or are you going to serve it in cups?" Aaron questioned.

For a split second Anna didn't understand what he was referring to, but then she exclaimed, "Oh! I almost forgot about that! The first time I invited Aaron over for Saturday night supper with *Daed* and Naomi, I made this pie—do you remember, Roy and Raymond? I was so nervous I forgot to put in cornstarch and I doubled the cream. No matter how much I beat it, the mixture wouldn't thicken, but I put it in the oven and hoped for the best."

"It was runnier than that gravy!" Ray chortled, pointing to Evan's half-eaten bowl of stew.

Anna giggled into her napkin. "*Jah*, but if I recall correctly, that didn't stop Aaron from eating his entire serving! He said he wanted a spoon so he could get every last drop."

"I was trying to make a *gut* impression on your *daed* and Naomi," he confessed.

"I have to give you credit for that, especially because of the stomachache you endured for two days afterward," Anna said, catching her breath.

She remembered how her father's eyes had twinkled when he'd come home from work and confided to her and Naomi that Aaron spent the better part of the following Monday morning locked inside the men's washroom. Picturing her father's amusement as she conveyed the anecdote made Anna smile from ear to ear.

"You've become a much better cook since then," Aaron said through a mouthful of pie.

"Denki," Anna said. "At least, I haven't poisoned anyone lately, have I, Fletcher?"

She reached for his hand beneath the table but he pushed back his chair and dropped his napkin on his plate. "I need some fresh air," he said. "Eli and Evan, do you want to go turtle hunting down at the creek with me?"

The three of them were out the door before Anna had time to put the leftovers away.

* * *

Fletcher took such long strides the boys had to run to keep up. He could hear Anna calling him from a distance, but he didn't stop until Evan said, "Fletcher, I think Anna wants to *kumme*, too. We're supposed to wait whenever she calls us."

He stopped abruptly but didn't turn around to watch her approach. When he heard footsteps and the rustle of her skirt behind him, he resumed walking.

She instructed the boys, "I'm going to walk with Fletcher and I'd like the two of you to give us our privacy. You may run up ahead of us, but what's the rule at the creek?"

"We have to stay ten steps back from the edge unless an adult is present," they droned, before sprinting down the hill.

"Are you trying to stay ten steps away from *me*?" she breathlessly called to Fletcher, who slowed his pace slightly.

"Do you want me to?" he asked.

"Of course not! Why would I want that?"

Fletcher didn't mince words. "You seemed to be standing very close to Aaron when I came in. I thought perhaps your *preferences* had changed."

Anna grabbed his wrist, pulling him to a complete stop. Her brows formed a severe line across her forehead as she glowered at him. "Whatever are you talking about, Fletcher?"

"I'm talking about the fact you spent the evening playing cards with him yesterday. You sent him a personal invitation this morning. You were practically standing nose-to-nose with him when I walked in this evening. You made his favorite dessert for supper. And you spent the entire meal reliving your courtship. *That's* what I'm talking about!" he ranted.

Anna didn't so much drop his wrist as flung it at him before she wordlessly tromped down the hill.

"Is that your response?" Fletcher shouted after her. "You have nothing to say?"

Twirling around, she glared at him and shouted back, "Believe me, you wouldn't want to hear the things I might say if I didn't hold my tongue at this moment. Besides, I've lost sight of the boys and I need to make sure they're okay."

Although he was seething, Fletcher followed her at a distance, also concerned about the boys' safety. After cutting through the woods, he spotted them overturning rocks along the upper embankment. Anna was watching from her roost on the boulder. Fletcher picked up a handful of pebbles and tarried midway between Anna and the boys, aimlessly chucking the stones one by one into the water.

"I think if there are any turtles here, they've gone in for the night," Eli hollered.

"*Jah*, probably," Fletcher called back. "They like warm sunshine, not cool evening air. But the frogs might be out. See if you can sneak up on one of them."

While the boys dropped to their knees in the grass, Fletcher ambled over to where Anna was sitting and leaned against the far edge of the same boulder. Her profile was set like concrete as she gazed across the creek and spoke in a controlled monotone.

"The card game, the invitation, the special dinner—it was all because I referred to Aaron as a pig yesterday. I was trying to make amends. When you entered the parlor before dinner, I'd just finished apologizing. You can ask Melinda and Aaron if you don't believe me."

Feeling like a fool, Fletcher said, "That won't be necessary, Anna. I believe you."

"Really?" Her nostrils flared as she faced him. "Because I've told you repeatedly I don't have feelings for Aaron, yet you keep accusing me of—"

"It's not an accusation, Anna," Fletcher interrupted. His throat burned as he admitted, "It's... I don't know. I guess it's some kind of nagging concern on my part."

"But I keep telling you there's no reason for such concern."

Fletcher hesitated. He knew he was in dangerous territory but if he didn't voice his complaint now, it would resurface in his thoughts and affect his relationship with Anna until he did. "But you really did seem to cherish recalling your courtship with Aaron tonight."

Anna threw her hands into the air and then slapped them against her lap. "What I cherished recalling was a happy memory of my *daed*, not of Aaron!"

Just then one of the boys let out a tremendous shriek. Anna and Fletcher sprang from the boulder and whipped around: the noise had come from behind them.

"He yanked my hand really, really hard!" Evan wailed, purple-faced and sobbing.

"He wouldn't *kumme* when I told him to," Eli tattled.

Anna crouched to examine the mark on the back of Evan's hand where Eli had grabbed it and then she lifted it to her lips and blew on it before giving his skin a kiss. "I know it hurts," she said. "But you'll survive. Why don't you go search that patch of grass over there to see what kinds of creatures you can find?"

Then she took Eli by the shoulders and looked into his eyes. "What has your *mamm* taught you about using your voice instead of your hands to express yourself?"

"But he was spying on you and Fletcher and you said you wanted privacy!" Eli blubbered. "Terrible things happen when you spy and I didn't want you to get hurt again!"

As Anna pulled the sobbing child to her chest and patted his back, she sent Fletcher a quizzical look and he shrugged in return, their own argument momentarily suspended. When Eli was quieted again, Anna took his hands in hers and asked, "What do you mean, you don't want me to get hurt again?"

Eli shook his head. "I can't tell you."

Anna lifted Eli's hands and gave them a small shake for emphasis. "I promise you, no matter what you say, you won't be punished for telling the truth. Do you know something about my accident? Is that what you meant about me getting hurt again?"

The boy nodded and a few more tears bounced off his round cheeks.

"Eli, it's very important you tell me."

Eli sucked his bottom lip in and out as he confessed, "I was spying on you and Aaron at the creek the night before your accident. People can get hurt when other people eavesdrop or repeat gossip, that's what *Mamm* and you always tell me, but I did it anyway and then the next day you got injured. I'm sorry, Anna. I'm really, really sorry."

Fletcher felt as if he'd been walloped in the abdomen with a fifty-pound sack of feed. The night before Anna's accident was a Monday; he remembered because he was personally extending wedding invitations to people outside their church, as was the Amish custom in their district. What were Anna and Aaron doing at the creek together?

"Shh, shh, shh," Anna shushed Eli, enfolding him in her arms. "You were very brave to tell me the truth, but I promise you, Eli, it wasn't your fault I hurt my head."

"Neh," Fletcher confirmed, peeling Eli out of Anna's grasp. "It wasn't your fault at all and this one time, it's okay to repeat what you heard when you were eavesdropping. So I want you to think hard, Eli. What were Anna and Aaron talking about at the creek?"

Anna straightened into a standing position. "Why are you asking him that? He's a *kind*. I'm sure he can't remember what two adults were talking about, much less understand the context—"

"Do you?" Fletcher was squatting on the balls of his feet next to Eli as he stared into the child's eyes. "Do you remember what Anna and Aaron were talking about?"

"Neh." Eli shook his head. "I wasn't close enough to hear. I only saw them kissing and then *Mamm* called me home from up the hill."

The boy's reply staggered Fletcher and he landed on his backside, too stunned to speak or move.

"It's getting dark." Anna felt light-headed and her voice trembled. "Eli and Evan, I'd like you boys to go directly into the house and tell Melinda or Raymond or Roy that Anna said one of them is to draw a bath for you. Fletcher and I will follow you from a distance."

After the boys scurried into the woods, Anna extended her hand to Fletcher, but he pushed it out of his way. He stood up of his own volition and smacked the dirt from the back of his trousers before striding after the boys.

"Fletcher!" Anna called. Her legs felt as if they were made of pudding and she struggled to keep up. "I don't know what Eli thought he saw, but you can't possibly take it seriously. He's a *kind*. He doesn't know what he's talking about."

Fletcher pivoted and marched back toward her, his eyes ablaze. "You're right, Eli is a *kind*, so I can't trust his interpretation of events. And you have amnesia, so I can't trust yours, either, can I? However, there is *one* person who knows for certain what happened that Monday night and although I've never found him to be entirely reliable, this time I'll have to take him at his word!"

"*Neh!*" Anna pleaded, tugging on his arm. "You can't ask Aaron that."

"Why not, Anna? Because you don't want me to find out the truth—is that it?"

"*Neh*, because it's so false as to be *narrish!*" Anna negated the notion, referring to it as crazy. "Besides, you'll upset the *kinner* if you go tearing into the house like a rabid dog! Eli has been bearing the guilt of my accident for weeks. That's probably why he's had such terrible stomachaches. Do you want to upset him further? You know how that will affect Naomi! And what about Melinda? How will she feel if you accuse her fiancé of kissing me?"

Fletcher shook Anna's hand from his forearm. "She'll feel devastated, the same way I feel now—but it's better if she knows the truth before she marries Aaron."

Anna charged up ahead of Fletcher so she could angle to face him as he approached. "It doesn't have to be that way, Fletcher. You don't have to feel devastated and neither does Melinda. The only reason you feel that way is because you've already decided I'm guilty. You're not giving me the benefit of the doubt!"

"I've been giving you the benefit of the doubt

since the moment I received the note from you, Anna. I've been hoping and praying and believing it didn't mean what I thought it meant. I convinced myself—*you* convinced me—that there had to be some kind of logical explanation. It had to be some kind of mistake," he sputtered.

For a moment Anna thought he was going to cry, but instead he stopped talking. When he spoke again, his volume was subdued. "I want to believe Eli is mistaken more than I've ever wanted anything in my life. But until we talk to Aaron about it, I'll always have a doubt in my mind."

"Okay, fine," she conceded. "We'll talk to him—but outside, just the three of us. Not where the *kinner* or Melinda can hear."

When they got within sight of the house, they noticed Roy heading indoors with the milk pail, so they asked him to send Aaron outside to the barn. While they were waiting, Anna lifted her apron to wipe her face, and then smoothed the fabric back into place, unable to look Fletcher in the eye. A second later, she heard the house door slamming, followed by the patter of footfall.

"I have a direct question for you and I expect the absolute truth," Fletcher said frankly when Aaron stood before them near the side of the barn. "Did you and Anna kiss the day before her accident?"

Aaron jerked his head backward and then a bemused smirk snaked across his lips. "You remembered?" he asked Anna, and immediately Fletcher kicked the side of the barn so forcefully the cows inside lowed.

Overcome with disbelief, Anna closed her eyes until the spinning sensation stopped. By the time she opened them, Fletcher had left. Her fists clenched, she snarled at Aaron, "Get out of my way." When he stepped aside, she rushed across the yard to where Fletcher was unhitching his horse from the post.

"Perhaps the kiss didn't mean what you think it means," she said. She was nearly on her knees, pleading for him to consider other possibilities. "Things aren't always as they appear to be—"

"Stop!" Fletcher directed, holding up his hand. "Enough is enough! The kiss means exactly what I think it means and so does your note. I can accept the truth, but now it's time—it's *past* time—for you to admit it."

"And what truth is that?"

Fletcher glanced toward the back door of the house, waiting until Aaron went inside again. "You still love Aaron," he hissed.

Anna's mouth twisted as she cried openly. "But I don't. I'm telling you, Fletcher, I don't love him. May the Lord forgive me, but most of the time I don't even *like* him."

"The facts say otherwise."

"They aren't facts. They're perceptions. Erroneous perceptions," she sobbed. "I don't know how to explain what happened the day before my accident, but I do know what it feels like to be betrayed and I would never, ever do that to anyone, especially you."

"Perhaps not willingly, not consciously, but you don't know your own heart, Joyce."

The slip of his tongue wasn't lost on Anna. "I do, too, know my own heart. I know it far better than you do," she contradicted, "and my name is Anna, not Joyce."

"*Jah*, but you're sure acting a lot like she did."

Anna shook her head sadly, slowly backing away. She choked out the words, "I can't marry a man who doesn't trust me."

"And I can't marry a woman I can't trust," Fletcher retorted as he climbed into his buggy.

Clasping her hands over her mouth, Anna fled to the house. When she got inside, she sailed past the dirty dishes still on the table, avoided the sitting room where Aaron and the older boys were taking out the cards for a game of Dutch Blitz and ignored Melinda's request for assistance above the sound of sloshing water in the washroom. As far as Anna was concerned, the entire household could collapse around her. She was tired of helping them: at this moment, she was the one who needed help. In her bedroom, she threw herself to her knees beside her bed, but found she couldn't say a word to the Lord. Instead, she poured out her heart in the form of rasping sobs, knowing He'd understand.

It was a good thing the horse often traveled the route between Anna's house and his, because Fletcher was so angry he couldn't see straight, and the animal was guided more by habit than by Fletcher's hand. He hardly recalled stabling the horse and walking into the house, but once inside, he paced from room to room, attempting to make sense of the events that had just unfolded. No matter how desperately he tried to allow for the possibility that all was not lost, he kept circling back to the same conclusion: Anna loved Aaron. Or, at the very least, she felt conflicted enough to kiss him only one day after publicly announcing her engagement to Fletcher. In either case, the wedding was off. Their *marriage* was off. Their bond was broken.

Asking himself how this situation could possibly be happening again, he reflected on his early days with Anna. After what he'd been through with Joyce Beiler, he could scarcely believe it when God blessed him with the type of relationship he shared with Anna. She had been trusting, open, good-humored and gracious beyond measure. Until he met her, he hadn't really known what love was—and not just the love he had for her, but the love she reciprocated toward him. The connection they shared grew stronger every day until he was certain it wouldn't just endure throughout their lifetime; it would flourish. But he'd been wrong.

Raking his hand through his hair, he spotted his wedding suit carefully arranged on a hanger that was hooked to a peg on the wall of the parlor. He'd put it there the day after kissing Anna for the first time since her accident. It was meant to remind him to focus on the future. But now the suit's form seemed to mock how lifeless he felt internally and he lunged toward it, swiping it from the peg and hurling it to the floor, where it lay in a crumpled heap like the rest of his dreams.

He kicked it aside and smacked the heel of his hand against the outer wall of the alcove. Then he did the same with the opposite hand. The force of his blows left two cracked dents in the plasterboard, but he was so embittered he swung his foot, putting a third hole in the wall before dropping backward onto the sofa. The damaged wall looked like two eyes and a serious mouth staring disapprovingly at him, so he quickly jumped to his feet and stormed out of the house.

Unaware of where he was going, Fletcher only

knew he couldn't sit still. He trekked long into the night, ruminating about what would come next. Unfortunately, he knew from experience that he and Anna would need to meet with the deacon before announcing publicly that they'd called the wedding off. As for the humiliation that would follow, he supposed some might think he'd be better equipped to handle it the second time around, since he knew what to expect. But instead, he felt doubly mortified. Not only would he have to bear the disgrace of his broken engagement in Willow Creek, but word would travel to Green Lake, where he imagined he'd become something of a laughingstock.

Sniggering bitterly, he realized he was running out of places to go to escape the humiliation of being jilted. Nevertheless, he'd have to find somewhere else to live and work. He'd finish up the project they were working on now and give Isaiah and Aaron time to find another crew member to replace him, but then he was going to move on. There was no way he could continue to work for his cousin: it was only by the grace of God he hadn't verbally unleashed his fury on Aaron back at the barn. He knew what the Bible said about forgiveness and anger, yet he also knew what it said about fleeing temptation. Given the option, Fletcher thought it was wise to make himself scarce as soon as possible.

As he ambled up the lane to his own yard again, he realized he'd probably have to forfeit the house to Aaron and Melinda. Or worse, to Aaron and Anna. Crossing the grass, Fletcher tried to convince himself that the tears in his eyes were due to spring allergies and he wiped his face with the back of his sleeve. Still too distraught to sleep, he took out his tools and supplies and began repairing the holes he'd made in the wall. By the time he was finished, the sun was just peeking over the horizon and he was finally exhausted. He laid down on his bed fully dressed and was asleep before he had a chance to remove his shoes.

He woke to a loud banging on the door. Although he had no idea what time it was, he guessed from the sunlight flooding the room that it was after ten or eleven o'clock. *That better not be Aaron coming to lecture me for being late to work*, he thought.

When he tugged open the door, he was surprised to see his uncle. Had Aaron told him about what happened the previous night? Was that why he was here?

"*Onkel* Isaiah, *kumme* in," Fletcher said. "I… I wasn't feeling my best last night so I decided to sleep in. I'm late for work."

"*Jah*, I can see that," he noted. "I'll put on a pot of *kaffi* while you wash up."

After shaving, Fletcher emerged from the washroom. His uncle was in the alcove, examining the built-in bookshelf and opening and closing the built-in drawers on the interior wall. Extending a mug to Fletcher, Isaiah made a sweeping motion with his hand and said, "This is the finest design and craftsmanship I've ever seen from someone your age—your *daed* trained you well. Anna must be delighted."

Fletcher swallowed. So, Aaron hadn't told his father about last evening's debacle after all. Then why was Isaiah calling on him? "She hasn't seen it yet," he replied. "It's supposed to be a surprise."

"How is she doing?" Isaiah inquired cordially.

"She's healing slowly but surely," Fletcher answered. Until Anna and Fletcher met with the deacon, he decided he'd keep the news of the breakup to himself.

"That's *gut*," Isaiah continued. "You've probably been under a lot of financial pressure, what with her injury and medical bills and the work of preparing the house for her to move into it, including making these renovations?"

Fletcher was puzzled by what his uncle was getting at. "*Jah*, I was," he answered without elaborating.

"That must be costly," Isaiah commented, appearing to read Fletcher's reaction.

Fletcher wondered if his uncle had come to discuss his wages. "I try to be a *gut* steward with my resources," he said. "*Gott* always provides."

Isaiah didn't seem to hear him. His uncle's posture was so stiff and his skin so ashen, Fletcher wondered if he was ill. But he reasoned Isaiah would have gone directly home from work if he was sick. Besides, how did his uncle even know he could find Fletcher here instead of at the job site? Had Aaron or Roy or Raymond told him?

Isaiah pulled at his beard, finally stating gravely, "There is no easy way to approach this subject, so I will be direct. I have been looking over our accounts and there are some discrepancies."

"Discrepancies?" Fletcher echoed, confused. "What kind of discrepancies?"

"We have an unexplained deficit of nearly two thousand dollars," his uncle explained.

Fletcher whistled. "That's a lot. Could there be a mistake?"

"I have repeatedly tried to reconcile it myself."

"I see. I'm very sorry to hear that and I'd like to help you, *Onkel*, but aside from using a measuring tape, math and numbers have never been strengths of mine."

"*Neh*, son, I don't want you to look over the account," Isaiah said, his ears purpling. "I—I want to know if you know anything about this matter."

Suddenly the real concern behind Isaiah's comments about medical bills and the expense of making renovations to the house came clear. Fletcher felt as if his uncle had clocked him over the head with a wrench.

"While it's true I've occasionally signed off on the company account—under Aaron's direction—or used the bank card to purchase supplies or withdraw cash for our work projects, I've always provided him the receipts," Fletcher declared. "I don't know anything about this matter."

His uncle took him by the shoulders and looked him in the eye. "I believe you, Fletcher, but it was only fair and right for me to ask. Now drink your *kaffi* and then make yourself some eggs. You look like you could use a little nourishment."

But after the door clicked shut behind Isaiah, Fletcher was too nauseated to eat. He hadn't thought it was possible to feel more betrayed than he'd felt when he confirmed Anna kissed Aaron, but once again, he was wrong. Having his own uncle accuse him of thievery was an indignity greater than he could bear. Setting his hat on his head, he decided then and there that he'd return to work alright—but only long enough to tell Aaron he quit. Then he was packing up his things and leaving immediately. He couldn't get away from Willow Creek fast enough.

Chapter Ten

After her *daed* died, Anna discovered one of the horrible truths about grieving: no matter how many tears she shed, her eyes never ran dry. It was as if her body had an unlimited capacity to mourn. She found this truth returning to her as she soaked her pillow with sadness the morning after her argument with Fletcher, just as she'd done the previous night.

There was a tap on the door and Anna sat up. Her eyelids were so swollen she practically had to pry them open with her fingertips, but since the shades were drawn she hoped her stepmother wouldn't notice she'd been crying. *"Guder mariye,"* she said as Naomi entered with a tray of tea, cheese and fruit.

"You mean *guder nammidaag*," Naomi replied. "How are you feeling?"

"Groggy, but otherwise alright. I'm sorry. I really overslept."

"*Neh*, I don't mean how are you feeling physically, Anna dear. Clearly something is troubling you and I'd like to help."

Anna was moved by Naomi's expression of compassion. Knowing she could disclose even her deepest heartaches to her stepmother, Anna confided what transpired the evening before and the decision she and Fletcher had made. She managed to get through most of the details without weeping, but when she started to sniff, Naomi moved to wrap an arm around her shoulders.

When Anna finished speaking, Naomi exhaled heavily. "I'm disappointed," she said. "Very, very disappointed."

"I know, Naomi. You've put so much work into preparing the house and—"

"*Neh!*" She clarified, "I'm not disappointed for my sake. I'm disappointed for yours. Quite frankly, I'm disappointed in Fletcher. I thought he was more mature than that."

Anna was surprised to hear herself defending him. "But, Naomi, as difficult as it is for me to believe it myself, there's very little question that I kissed Aaron. It's no wonder Fletcher is upset."

"Upset, *jah*. But Fletcher knows your character, just as I know your character, and I sense a piece of this puzzle is still missing—especially because Aaron is involved."

Anna took a napkin from the tray and blew her nose with it. "It hardly matters anymore. Fletcher and I have made up our minds. I suppose we'll have to talk to the deacon before we tell the *leit* from church that the wedding is off. We'll want to notify our out-of-state guests as soon as possible, too. I guess we'll call them from the phone shanty, so they can cancel their travel plans. But I don't know how or what I'm going to tell Melinda. I don't think she has any clue about what happened last night."

Naomi patted Anna's shoulder. "You shouldn't concern yourself with those matters right now. Melinda's wedding is still almost three weeks away. You needn't tell her anything right now. Today, you need all the rest you can get. Your head will be clearer tomorrow."

"*Jah*, since I don't have to keep up with my own wedding preparation schedule anymore, I'll take a leisurely walk down to the creek."

"That sounds like a *gut* idea," Naomi replied as she stood to leave. "It's a beautiful spring day. Just be careful not to slip on any rocks."

By the time Anna finished picking at the plate of food Naomi had brought her, got dressed and journeyed to the creek, she felt so fatigued she wished she were back in bed. Her lethargy was more emotional than physical: every thought she had was of her breakup with Fletcher. Closing her eyes, she reclined on the boulder and tried to concentrate on the warmth of the sun on her skin, the smell of damp earth and the sound of water cascading over the stones. But it was no use: she kept envisioning the shocked look on Fletcher's face when Eli announced he'd seen her and Aaron kissing.

Hearing a rustle coming from the direction of the park, she snapped her eyelids open and pushed herself upright. At first, she could only spy a dark head of hair through an opening of the trees and her breath quickened: it was Fletcher! But then the figure rounded the bend and she realized her mistake. The man's build was stocky and short, not lanky and tall.

"What are you doing here?" she demanded to know.

"*Guder nammidaag* to you, too," Aaron replied. "I've *kumme* to talk to you about what happened when we kissed. I wanted to tell you that you mustn't blame yourself."

Anna shielded her face with her hands to hide her humiliation. Her stomach was turning upside down and she wished Aaron would just vanish, but it sounded as if he was about to apologize and the least she could do was hear him out.

Instead, he patted her shoulder and said, "I

know you can't remember it now, but initially you were taken in by Fletcher because you were grieving and he provided a shoulder to cry on."

Anna shook her head. "*Neh*, that's not true," she contradicted.

Aaron persisted, "When he offered to walk out with you, you accepted in order to get back at me for dating Melinda. I confess, I was only feigning interest in her to hasten you to marry me because you'd been putting off the decision for so long. The entire situation had gotten completely out of hand, like a prank that had gone too far. But by the time we came to our senses, you had already agreed to marry Fletcher and I had proposed to Melinda."

"*Neh*." She panted, rising from the rock and spinning to face him. "*Neh*, it wasn't like that. My relationship with Fletcher had nothing to do with you."

"You don't remember, but it did. You as much as told me so yourself, when we discussed the matter under this very tree the day before your accident, the day we kissed," Aaron murmured, inching closer. "You said the charade had gone on long enough. Even though I was conflicted about breaking Melinda's heart, you insisted that I tell her how I really felt. I have to believe that was because you wanted me back."

"*Neh*," Anna repeated, although some small

part of what he was saying struck a chord deep in her memory. Her eyes began to spill and she swiped her cheek against her shoulder. "That's not right. It can't be."

"*Jah*, it is. But the next morning, you suffered your concussion and since then, you've never been able to recall what we discussed here, have you?"

"I've forgotten, but—"

"After a few weeks, it was clear to me your memory of our conversation would never return, even though I dropped as many hints about how we still felt about each other as I could. Since you were intent on marrying Fletcher, it seemed wrong for me to interfere, especially because Melinda and I had pressed forward with our own wedding plans."

Anna covered her ears to block out Aaron's words but he pulled her hands away and gripped them in his own.

"The other night, playing cards, we had such a *wunderbaar* evening together, like old times. You can't deny it," he insisted. "And now, Fletcher finally knows the truth… I think *Gott* may have brought us back together, Anna. I think it's time we acknowledge we've been His intended for each other all along."

"It was you, not Fletcher!" Anna squawked, suddenly understanding the memory she had of a man kissing her beneath the willow there at the creek. So *that* was why the feelings associated with it were so disturbing to her!

"Exactly, it was me you loved, not Fletcher," Aaron cooed, wrapping his arms around her trembling shoulders and whispering into her ear. "Now you've got it."

"Neh," she threatened. "Now *you're* going to get it if you don't let go of me this instant and get out of my sight."

Aaron stepped back and his mouth dropped open as if he was about to retort, but Anna screwed her face into the most menacing look she could muster and he left without uttering another syllable. Then, she picked up a stone and lobbed it into the current. *I knew I wouldn't have voluntarily kissed Aaron!* she thought. *I knew it!* But her discovery was of little satisfaction: even if she set the record straight by telling Fletcher what happened, he already admitted he didn't trust her. *If he really knew and loved me, he would have trusted me no matter what Aaron had said*, she thought.

She stumbled back to the boulder, where she lay covering her face with her hands and crying until her head began to ache, and she knew if she didn't stop she'd wind up in Dr. Donovan's office again. Squinting, she thought she saw something glinting overhead between the trunk and an arm of the willow. She circled the tree, craning her neck: there was definitely something up there. Like a flash of lightning, the phrase "squirrel it away in a secret place" occurred to her. That's what she'd told Fletcher she did with her journal!

She leaped up and grabbed hold of the bottom branch. However depleted she felt physically, she made up for it in sheer determination, hoisting herself over the limb in a burst of vigor. Once upright, she was an avid climber, ascending the branches as easily as a ladder. She wrenched the tin from its storage place and scampered back to the ground. Scraped raw, her fingers trembled as she pried the rusted tin open.

She removed the journal and pressed the cold leather to her cheek. Using the key from the string she'd worn around her neck ever since she'd learned the journal was missing, she could feel her heart thudding as she unclasped the lock and opened the diary to the first page. *This journal was given to me by Fletcher Chupp, what a heel*, it said.

Her tears were bittersweet as she ran up the hill to the house, clutching all that remained of her relationship with Fletcher to her heart.

When Fletcher arrived at the work site after lunch, he found Roy and Raymond working unsupervised. He didn't want them to hear what he had come to say to his cousin, so he planned to conduct his conversation outdoors. "Where's Aaron?" he asked.

"He was already here this morning when Melinda dropped us off," Roy reported. "But after he talked to her, he left again. It was too early for Melinda to go to the shop—the two of them probably sneaked off for *kaffi* and doughnuts somewhere."

Raymond rolled his eyes over Roy's head. "He also mentioned he had to run an errand," Raymond elaborated. "I wonder if he went with his *daed* to the lumber store to talk about the problem with the accounts."

"What do you know about the problem with the accounts?" Fletcher's ears perked up.

"Nothing," Raymond replied. "Only that Isaiah came here this morning and questioned Roy and me about a discrepancy."

"I told him I didn't know anything about it, either," Roy chimed in.

"We aren't even allowed to sign for anything," Raymond stated. "But Isaiah said as a matter of fairness he was asking each of us on the crew. He said he intended no offense, but he needed to check with us before making a major decision that would affect the responsible party."

"Jah," Roy agreed. "It sounds as if we may be taking our business to another lumber store

soon. Either that, or Aaron's really going to get an earful. It all depends on whose fault it was, I guess."

Ach, Fletcher realized, *Onkel wasn't singling me out!* Fletcher was absolutely dumbfounded. He had completely misread the situation. He'd been so indignant about what he deemed was Isaiah's unwarranted insinuation that he'd been ready to quit his job and abandon his family on the spot over the offense. But come to find out, Fletcher was the one in the wrong: Isaiah didn't mean what Fletcher thought he meant. "Things aren't always as they appear to be," Anna said the night before and Fletcher had scoffed at her for it.

Isaiah's words, "I believe you, Fletcher, but it was only fair and right for me to ask," echoed in his mind. Isaiah simply asked the question and accepted Fletcher's response immediately, regardless of how incriminating his financial circumstances may have appeared.

But had Fletcher demonstrated the same level of trust in Anna, the woman he claimed to love? No. On the contrary, he'd badgered her with repeated inquiries and then dismissed her answers anyway. He'd as much as said she was ignorant, if not lying, about her deepest feelings. The realization of how he'd failed her caused his heart to spasm with a searing pain. He had to apologize.

He had to beg her forgiveness and keep begging it until she accepted his apology.

"Are you alright?" Raymond asked.

"*Neh*, I'm not," Fletcher answered. "I have to leave immediately. If Aaron returns, tell him… tell him I'm not coming in for the rest of the day."

Before he could see Anna, there was a present Fletcher wanted to buy, something he'd seen in the gift shop at the medical center in Highland Springs. He wasted no time journeying there, and when he arrived he hastily hitched the horse in the adjoining lot and hustled toward the building. He made his purchase inside and was about to exit when a familiar form breezed through the door.

"Fletcher!" Dr. Donovan's voice reverberated. "You're not here visiting anyone, are you?"

"*Neh*. Just taking care of a personal matter. Getting a gift for Anna, actually."

"Glad to hear it. After what the two of you have been through, I wouldn't want any more challenges coming your way before the big day." He thrust his arm forward to shake hands with Fletcher. "Congratulations, son—and give that bride of yours my best wishes, too."

"Thank you, I will," Fletcher said. *Provided she's still talking to me.*

Realizing he hadn't changed his clothes since

the morning before, Fletcher stopped at home to put on a fresh shirt and pants before calling on Anna. He brushed his teeth and hair and was locking the door behind him when he noticed his uncle sitting on a bench on the porch.

"My knee aches—it must be going to rain tomorrow," Isaiah said by way of greeting.

Clearly his uncle had come back to discuss something more important than the weather, and Fletcher wished he'd let him know what it was because he needed to be on his way to Anna's house.

"I'm getting too old for the kind of work we do," Isaiah confided. "I'm definitely too old to have a son who behaves so irresponsibly. I had hoped by working with you every day, he'd pick up on some of your values and habits, but instead, he's only taken advantage of your scrupulous work ethic."

Fletcher couldn't deny the truth of what Isaiah was saying but neither did he think it prudent to confirm it, so he remained silent.

"What's more, he's made a mess of our orders and our accounts. His sloppiness nearly cost us our relationship with our supplier in the process. But I believe he can improve his abilities if he receives additional training under my tutelage," his uncle proposed. "I'd like him to work with me on our projects in the Highland Springs community."

Fletcher nodded, relieved that Isaiah seemed to have reconciled the deficit in the account. Although he imagined the demotion was disgruntling to his cousin, Fletcher marveled at Isaiah's forbearance toward Aaron. Anna's words, "People change. They grow. With *Gott*'s help, we all do," ran through Fletcher's mind as he realized his uncle still carried that kind of loving hope for his son. Fletcher prayed Anna would see Fletcher's own potential for change and growth, too.

Isaiah continued, "What this means, however, is I'll need a reliable, knowledgeable foreman to handle our *Englisch* clients and to supervise the crew. Raymond is too inexperienced to be a foreman, although he'll get a pay raise. Eventually Roy will, too, if he keeps progressing like he is... Anyway, what do you say? Will you accept the position of foreman?"

Denki, Lord, Fletcher prayed.

"The promotion would mean a raise for you, too, of course," Isaiah offered, prompting Fletcher to his senses.

"*Jah*, of course I will accept the position," he confirmed. "*Denki, Onkel* Isaiah, *denki!*"

"You're the one I should be thanking," Isaiah stated. "You're unfailingly dependable, just like your *daed* always was. But that doesn't mean you don't need a hand yourself. I've been worried about the emotional and financial burden you've been carrying ever since Anna's injury. I understand there were back taxes to pay on the house, too. If you need help, that's what family is for, Fletcher. Just ask."

Fletcher further understood that when his uncle was questioning him about his expenses, it wasn't because Isaiah was accusing him; it was because Isaiah was *concerned* about him.

"*Denki*, I will," Fletcher replied.

Before doddering down the steps, his uncle handed him an envelope. "This is from your *groossdaadi*. I don't know what it says, but he asked me to give it to you in the event your wedding was published in church this spring. Because of the chaos following Anna's accident, I'm sorry to say I forgot all about it until now."

Fletcher waited until he'd embarked his buggy to tear open the envelope. The note read:

To Fletcher J. Chupp,
If you are reading this, it means the lovely Anna Weaver has agreed to become your wife—an answer to my prayers. Although the two of you may have thought you were keeping your courtship a secret, nothing could have been more obvious to me than your mutual fondness, respect and loyalty.

It was a delight to spend the last part of my life witnessing the kind of young love that reminded me of my own courtship with your grandmother so many years ago.

Although you both suffered painful betrayals, I'm glad you've decided not to allow past hurts to rob you of future hopes and present happiness. As I've discovered this last year in particular, time passes too quickly, so be sure to keep your heart open to love.

May you, Anna and your family experience God's grace and blessings in your new home.

From Elmer J. Chupp.

Fletcher folded the letter and tucked it beneath the seat. Emboldened by its message, he flicked the reins, working the horse into a rapid gallop. He didn't have a minute to spare.

Anna could hear the distant clatter of pots and pans as Melinda fixed dinner, and she was glad for once she didn't have to participate in the meal preparation. As soon as she returned from the creek, Anna had secured Naomi's promise that her stepmother wouldn't allow anyone to disturb her, and she sequestered herself in her attic room, perusing her diary page by page.

As she read, she rediscovered many of the events Fletcher had already described to her, but many more she had no idea had ever happened. Whether she'd written about a picnic by Wheeler's Pond, reuniting with Fletcher after the tornado struck, or even a small argument over what time they arranged to meet after church, one theme consistently ran throughout the entries: she was in love.

Placing the open book on her stomach as she reclined in bed, Anna realized she didn't need her journal to tell her that. She knew she'd fallen in love with Fletcher all over again because breaking up with him didn't merely split her heart in two; it smashed it into a million bits. A few tears trickled down her temples before she picked up the journal and turned the page. A folded sheet of paper fell to her chest.

The entry in the journal where the letter was tucked was dated January 12 and it said, *Today Naomi gave me the enclosed letter, which she only just discovered hidden in Dad's Bible on his lamp stand. Although it's nearly a year old, I'm so glad to have received it now. I'll treasure it always.*

Unfolding the paper, Anna gasped at the sight of her father's lopsided penmanship. His letter was dated February 18 of the previous year.

My darling Daughter,

Tonight I stood at the bottom of the attic stairs, as I have every evening this week, listening to you weeping in your room where you thought no one could hear you. I am torn between wanting to comfort you and respecting your privacy (which you have always fiercely guarded, much to your brothers' chagrin!).

As difficult as it is to know you're suffering, I don't believe Aaron is the Lord's intended for you. He has his admirable qualities to be sure, but he lacks the sense of responsibility, selflessness and genuine kindness you deserve. If Aaron possessed those qualities, you would have married him long ago.

Instead, I believe you've continued to allow him to court you in an effort to model the characteristics he ought to have developed by now. I see you exhibiting the same gentle patience with Melinda that you've always shown to Aaron. But ultimately, such growth has to come from inside them, through the grace of God, as it does for all of us.

I wish I could take away your heartache, but I trust God will use it for your good. It is my prayer He will provide you a husband who brings you joy instead of grief—perhaps even joy in the midst of grief. When you meet a man like that, you can be certain he is God's intended for you.

Your loving Father.

Anna's heart palpitated as she replaced the letter and turned the page of her journal to the next entry, dated January 19. It read: *Fletcher asked me to marry him and I eagerly accepted. He was willing to wait until wedding season next autumn, but I want to become his wife as soon as possible, so we will take advantage of the bishop's special spring wedding provision and marry on the first available date in April. Nothing would make me more grateful than having him as my husband by Easter.*

There it was, in black and white, the explanation she'd been seeking for why she had been certain after such a brief courtship that Fletcher was God's intended for her. It was what her father wrote about finding a man who brought her joy in the midst of grief that must have helped her to be sure... *But it does me no gut now*, she lamented.

She knew she could show Fletcher the journal. She could flip to the last entry, as she'd already done and insist that he read her words, dated Monday, March 2: *Tonight, Aaron told me he never loved Melinda—he was only courting her to try to make me jealous. Then he kissed me and I was so angry, I would have liked to push him into the creek, may the Lord forgive me! I pleaded with him to confess the charade to Melinda before the wedding preparations went any further, but he refused. I don't know what to do, except to tell Fletcher. He'll know how best to handle it.*

But even if Fletcher saw the error in his thinking this time, Anna knew that at some point in the future, an issue or circumstance would arise in which Fletcher would doubt her and she would feel burdened to prove herself again. She meant what she said; she couldn't marry a man who didn't trust her, no matter how much she loved him. The tears flowed freely and she rolled onto her side and burrowed her face into her pillow.

She had nearly cried herself to sleep when she heard a tap at the window. At first she thought it must be the maple tree's branches blowing in the wind, but when suddenly it scraped the pane again, she wondered if it was a bird or a squirrel. She heard it scratch the glass a third time, louder now, as if it were deliberately trying to enter the house. She crossed the room and slid the window open, peering into the maple, which was leafy with new growth.

"Scat," she rebuked the concealed animal. "Go away. Get!"

"Anna, is that you?" a man's voice called softly.

"Who's there?" she questioned, although she realized it had to be Aaron. He hadn't been permitted to visit Melinda at suppertime, so he must have been sneaking to speak with her now.

"It's me, Fletcher," he answered.

"Fletcher?" She was completely bewildered. "What in the world are you doing up here?"

"I'm… I'm going out on a limb for you, Anna," Fletcher chuckled awkwardly. "I've *kumme* to apologize."

Anna laughed. In the midst of her grief, Fletcher was bringing her joy. "But you're afraid of heights," she said.

"Naomi wouldn't let me inside to see you," he explained. "But, uh, I would like to get down now. Would you *kumme* outside?"

"I'll be right there," she agreed. She was so glad to see him that she made it downstairs and outside quicker than he descended the tree's branches, but she stopped short of embracing him when he dropped to the ground. She needed to hear his apology first.

"Hello again, Anna," he said, wiping his hands on the sides of his trousers.

"Hello again, Fletcher," she replied. She

started to suggest they go sit on the porch swing, but he gently placed a finger to her lips to silence her.

"Please, what I have to say can't wait another instant," Fletcher insisted. He dropped his hand and continued, "I don't know how to explain the note you sent me, or the kiss you and Aaron shared—"

"But I do," Anna interrupted. "It's all in my journal and I can show—"

"Neh!" Fletcher declared urgently. His eyes brimmed and his voice quavered as he explained, "What I wanted to say was I don't know how to explain those things, but I don't have to explain them, because I know *you*. You've always been truthful and trustworthy about your thoughts and feelings, and having amnesia doesn't change that. So when you told me those things didn't mean what I thought they meant, I should have believed you the first time. The fact that I doubted you is a reflection of my character, not yours. My lack of trust—my insecurity—is a weakness I hope *Gott* will change and you will forgive, because I'm very, very sorry."

Upon her hearing the depth of Fletcher's remorse and the intensity of his belief in her trustworthiness, Anna's wounded feelings evaporated and she was consumed by the yearning to be reconciled with him. She hurtled herself into his arms with such force she nearly knocked him over. "Of course I forgive you!" she exclaimed.

After they'd nearly hugged the breath right out of each other, Anna dropped her arms and said, "I need to ask you to forgive me, too. Your suspicion that Aaron still had feelings for me was correct. But because I didn't reciprocate even an ounce of that affection, I was completely blind to his behaviors and I dismissed your concerns. I'm sorry. Perhaps if I had been more aware—"

"I'm not eavesdropping," Evan announced loudly from where he stood by the side of the house. "*Mamm* sent me out here to see if you want any supper before they put the leftovers away, Anna."

Anna laughed. "*Jah*, please. I'll be in in a few minutes and Fletcher would like to join me, as well."

"Alright, if you want to," the boy said to Fletcher, ruefully shaking his head. "But Melinda made ground beef and cabbage skillet and it tastes even worse than it smells. Eli called it ground beef and *skunk cabbage* skillet!"

"Evan!" Anna scolded, but the child had already darted off.

"Are you sure it's okay if I *kumme* in for supper?" Fletcher asked. "Naomi didn't seem too happy to see me earlier."

"She'll be delighted now," Anna insisted. "So will Evan and Eli, since it will mean fewer of Melinda's leftovers for them tomorrow!"

Oh, how Fletcher had missed this kind of easygoing repartee the past few days. "Okay, but just don't tell Naomi I climbed the tree outside your window. She'll lecture me to no end."

"Well, I can't blame her for that—you could have slipped and gotten a concussion," Anna joked. "And I would have been devastated if you didn't remember me."

No sooner had she spoken the words than she clapped her hand over her mouth.

"That's how I injured myself!" she exclaimed. "I fell as I was letting myself down from the tree."

"You climbed the maple tree, too?" Fletcher wondered.

"*Neh*, the willow," Anna expounded. "I was letting myself down from the last branch, but my feet couldn't quite touch the ground. When I released my grip, I sort of floundered and then toppled backward. I remember bouncing onto my backside and thinking 'that wasn't so bad,' and then total darkness."

"You must have hit your head on a rock as you tumbled. But why were you climbing the tree in the first place? You weren't hiding, were you?"

"*Neh*, I wasn't hiding. Rather, I wasn't hiding myself. I was hiding my journal, which contained a terrible secret. You see, the day after our wedding intentions were published, Aaron came to me at the creek and confessed he never really loved Melinda. He'd only been trying to make me jealous, which didn't work, of course. I captured it all in my journal, even the part where he kissed me..." Anna shivered, making an awful face.

Fletcher felt his jaw harden and his temples pulsate, but he silently prayed, *Forgive us our trespasses as we forgive those who trespass against us.* If Anna could forgive Aaron for kissing her, he could, too.

She continued, "So actually, you were partially right when you thought the 'A.' in my note referred to Aaron. I did have serious concerns about him I needed to discuss with you before the wedding preparations went any further. But the wedding preparations I was referring to were Aaron and Melinda's, not ours!"

"Oh, Anna, I'm so sorry," Fletcher said.

"You've already apologized, Fletcher, and it's understandable why you might have thought what you thought, at least initially, so please say no more," Anna replied. "The important thing now is that Melinda needs to know the truth."

"*Jah*, but Aaron is the one who needs to tell her, not us. I'll have a word with him. Something tells me he won't want to risk getting in any more hot water with his *daed*. He'll own up, don't worry. Meanwhile—" Fletcher bent to retrieve the gift bag from where he'd left it propped against the tree "—this is for you."

"Denki," Anna said. She gingerly removed the colorful bouquet of tissue paper to retrieve the bag's contents: a leather-bound journal with a silver lock on the side and a willow tree embossed on the front cover. "It's beautiful!"

"But now that you've found yours, I guess you don't really need a second one."

"But I do!" she protested. "My old journal is nearly full. I can use this to record the next chapter of our lives together."

Fletcher lightly ran his knuckle beneath Anna's chin, tilting her face toward his. "I just hope the next chapter isn't as rocky as the past few weeks have been."

"Oh, but all *gut* love stories have a few rocky patches. That's how they get their beauty," Anna said. "I wouldn't change our story for anything in the world."

"Neither would I," Fletcher agreed as he searched her eyes. They had never appeared so dazzling.

"What is it?" she asked. "Why are you staring at me that way?"

"I haven't seen that look in your eyes for a long, long time," he whispered.

"It's a look of recognition," she whispered back, causing his heart to throb. "I know who you are. No matter what I may remember or forget about the past, I know who you are."

"Who am I?" he asked playfully.

"You're Fletcher Josiah Chupp—*Gott*'s intended for me."

"And you, Anna Catherine Weaver, are *Gott*'s intended for me," Fletcher pledged, pressing his forehead to hers.

"I love you," she murmured.

"And I love you," he echoed.

He could have stayed like that for hours, but when a breeze rustled the leaves overhead, Anna backed away. She smiled, revealing her dimple, and then linked her fingers with his. "*Kumme*, let's go inside. I can't wait to tell Naomi her faithful prayers have been answered!"

Epilogue

❧

Anna expected tears or even an outburst from Melinda the evening Aaron called off their wedding, but instead, the young woman almost seemed relieved.

"I enjoy working in the shop more than anything I've ever done," she told Anna, taking off her prayer *kapp* in preparation for bed. "But I'd have to quit working if I had a *bobbel* after I got married. Besides, once you move out, I'll have this entire room to myself. It will be a little bit like having a home of my own, without all of the work of a house."

"But aren't you sad about…about Aaron?" Anna carefully inquired.

"Why should I be sad? It's not his fault his salary was cut because he's no longer the foreman. His *daed* needs his personal help with their Highland Springs customers—it would be selfish of him to put marrying and building a costly house for me above his obligation to his *daed*." Melinda lowered her voice as if to reveal a great secret. "Isaiah's getting older, you know. He has *arthritis*."

"That's why Aaron told you he wanted to call off the wedding?" Anna asked, thoroughly astounded by his ability to concoct a tale that actually bore some semblance, however slight, to the truth. She found herself wondering if he ever truly intended to be so disingenuous, or if he simply was so optimistically self-deceived he didn't realize how distorted his perspective was. No matter: as Fletcher reminded her, it wasn't her place to set Aaron's record straight.

"*Jah,*" Melinda said as she ran a brush through her hair. "I told him I understood, but that I didn't know if I wanted to continue to walk out with him."

"Really?" Anna's eyebrows shot up.

"*Jah.*" She leaned forward and whispered. "Don't tell anyone I said this, but I heard that Joseph Schrock's nephew Jesse is coming to visit for the summer. He's about my age and by all counts, he's supposedly very charming."

Even after a year of living with Melinda, Anna still never knew what was going to come out of the young woman's mouth next, but she supposed in this instance, it was a good thing Melinda had such a fickle attention span: it seemed to have saved her from a world of hurt.

Anna slid her feet under her quilt. Soon, it would be too warm for such a heavy bed covering. "By the way, have you seen the fabric for my dress?" she asked. "I left it in the other side of the attic but it's missing and there's only about a week and a half until the wedding."

"*Neh.* But I thought you were supposed to be cured of amnesia." Melinda yawned.

"I *am* cured. Mostly, anyway. But there's a difference between the fabric being missing and forgetting where I put it. I'm telling you, it's not where I left it!"

"What's not where you left it?" Naomi asked. She'd crept up the stairs without Anna hearing her and she was standing in the doorway with her arms behind her back.

"My wedding dress fabric. I can't find it and I hardly have any time to sew my dress."

"That's because you spent too much time working on Melinda's dress, even though Dr. Donovan warned you to restrict your sewing activities."

Anna felt her face go warm as Melinda giggled. "I think that's the first time I've ever heard Naomi scold you, Anna!"

Anna playfully tossed a pillow at her cousin. "At least I'm being scolded for doing too much work instead of too little," she responded.

"Now, girls, do I have to separate you two?" Naomi teased, joining their laughter. She entered the room, displaying a deep green dress across one arm, and a dark purple dress on the other. "One for you, one for me, and Melinda's dress makes three."

Melinda and Anna both jumped out of their beds. Melinda darted to the closet while Anna approached Naomi and accepted her dress.

Holding it to her shoulders so it draped along the front of her figure, she looked down admiringly and said, "Oh, *denki*, Naomi. It's beautiful. Look—I can't even see the stitches they're so tiny!"

"Let's try them on, all three of us at once!" Melinda cried, sliding her own dress off its hanger.

"Melinda, you know that vanity is sinful," Naomi chastised.

"*Jah*, but we need to make sure they fit," Anna wheedled. "Please?"

"Not you, too, Anna!" Naomi clucked before agreeing it made sense that they should be certain no alterations were needed.

As soon as Melinda had changed, she twirled in a circle and asked her aunt, "What do you think?"

"It's a perfect fit," Naomi said carefully. "Anna did a very nice job sewing it for you."

Melinda's shoulders slumped and her lip jutted out. "But what do you think of how I look?"

Naomi blinked rapidly and wiped away a tear. "I think you look more and more like your lovely *mamm*—my sister—each day."

Melinda pranced to the mirror to view her reflection and Naomi turned toward Anna. In the soft glow of the lamp's light, Naomi appeared youthful and elegant, the lines of worry seemingly erased from her skin.

"I knew that color would be striking on you," Anna whispered. "I wish *Daed* could see you now."

"I wish he could see *you*," Naomi responded. "But when Fletcher gets a glimpse, you're going to set his heart aflutter!"

Anna threw her arms around Naomi, half crying, half laughing. "*Denki*, Naomi. *Denki* for sewing my dress and for your encouragement and for your prayers. *Denki* for everything!"

"There, there, we don't want to wrinkle our dresses," Naomi said, but instead of letting go, she squeezed Anna even tighter.

The wedding ceremony was everything Fletcher prayed it would be: he'd never been as certain of anything as he was when he answered "yes" to the bishop's four traditional wedding questions, especially the one about whether Fletcher was confident that the Lord had provided Anna as a marriage partner for him. Anna's voice rang out with an equally clear affirmation when the same question was posed to her about Fletcher.

The dinner following the three-hour sermon was especially bountiful, thanks to Naomi and also to his aunt and cousins, who generously shared their supply of celery for the traditional Amish wedding dishes, as well as other ingredients and foods they'd already begun preparing for Aaron's wedding. Tessa and Katie Fisher spent several days baking an excess of pies, cookies and other goodies. And, despite the short notice, Faith Yoder managed to deliver the most unusual wedding cake she said any bride—including Melinda—had ever requested: turtle cake.

To her credit, Melinda was a huge help on the day of the wedding. After the ceremony, she was in high spirits, flitting about the house in her violet dress and engaging the guests in conversation as if she were the bride herself. Although Aaron appeared forlorn at first, Fletcher later noticed him laughing with the young Emma Lamp in the parlor. As afternoon gave way to evening, Naomi and his aunt and cousins spread the tables with supper and more desserts, and the last local guests stayed until after ten o'clock.

Shortly after that, Fletcher readied his own buggy while Anna was inside saying her final goodbyes to Naomi and the rest of the overnight visitors. He'd just provided his faithful horse a carrot when the door swung open and his three sisters, Esther, Leah and Rebekah, emerged.

"You look disappointed. You must have been expecting Anna instead of us," Leah needled him. "She'll be right out."

"Are you getting impatient?" Esther asked.

"Neh," he answered. "I'll wait for Anna as long as it takes."

"Spoken like a man in love," Rebekah noted. "But you don't have to wait any longer, here *kummes* your bride now."

As Anna stepped outside, the light from the kitchen illuminated her silhouette. Although it was too dark to see her face, he could hear the smile in her voice when she said, *"Gut nacht,* everyone, and *denki.* See you tomorrow."

"Are you certain you don't want to spend the night at Naomi's house?" Fletcher asked when she was seated beside him. That was the customary Amish expectation of the bride and groom, because it enabled them to assist with the cleanup first thing in the morning.

"Just this once, I think we ought to do something irresponsible," Anna answered. Then she corrected herself. "Well, not irresponsible, since we'll *kumme* back to help bright and early, but something—"

"Out of character?" he asked.

"*Jah*. Besides, the house is bursting at the seams with out-of-state guests."

"That's true," Fletcher said. His pulse pounded louder and louder in his ears the closer they got to home. He couldn't wait to show Anna the alcove he'd created for her.

But when he brought the horse to a halt, she said, "Wait, before we step down, I have a gift for you. There wasn't really any way I could wrap it, so you have to take a look at it now. It's in the back seat, under the tarp."

"When did you have a chance to sneak a present back there?"

"I didn't," Anna replied, giggling. "Your *new-ehockers*, Chandler and Gabriel, put it in the buggy for me while I distracted you. Go ahead—see what it is."

Using the flashlight he kept secured to a hook in the front of his buggy to supply him with light, Fletcher twisted in the seat and lifted the tarp.

"A fishing rod!" he exclaimed. "*Denki*, Anna, it's a really nice one."

"Roy and Raymond told me that yours snapped the other day and I know how you enjoy fishing," she said. "You should be able to bring in a *gut* catch down at the creek using that rod."

"*Denki*," Fletcher repeated. "But *you're* my best catch, Anna."

Her laughter made light work of stabling the

horse and soon Fletcher was accompanying her to the house. He kissed her once on the cheek before he unlocked the kitchen door and led her down the hall in the dark.

Before illuminating the room in the alcove, he confessed, "I realize I said I didn't want either of us to feel as if we were hiding anything from each other, but there is one thing I admit I've been keeping a secret."

After Fletcher turned up the gas lamp, Anna blinked several times. Rendered completely speechless, she ran her hands over the shelves and opened each of the drawers before perching on the window seat.

"Fletcher, I don't know what to say," she cried. "I can't believe how beautiful this room is."

"I made it exclusively for you," he said. "So you'll have the space and privacy you need to read or write. There is one condition, however."

"Anything," she said.

"You can't use the room to write, *Fletcher Chupp, what a heel*, in your diary," he said softly into her ear.

"I accept the terms of the agreement," she pledged.

"Not *gut* enough," he replied. "You have to seal your promise with a kiss."

Leaning in, he gave her a firm, meaningful kiss. When he pulled away, he stared into her eyes, which were exquisitely enhanced by the green tint of her dress.

Suddenly, Anna clapped her hands against her cheeks as her eyes widened and her mouth dropped open. "Oh *neh*!" she exclaimed.

"What is it?"

"I think I may be suffering a relapse of amnesia. I can't recall what happened just now between us."

Fletcher threw back his head to laugh. "Don't worry," he consoled her. "I know how to jog your memory."

"With sage tea?" she flirted.

"Neh," he answered. "With this."

He feathered his lips across hers once, twice, three times before asking, "Is what happened coming back to you now?"

"Not quite," she teased. "It's still a bit hazy. But that's alright. As Dr. Donovan said, you and I have a lifetime to make memories together..."

Fletcher chuckled and wrapped his arms around her. A warm breeze wafted through the window: spring was definitely here, a season of hope, a season of renewal, a season of love. He and Anna were married at last.

* * * * *

*If you liked this story, pick up the
first book in Carrie Lighte's*
AMISH COUNTRY COURTSHIPS *series:*

AMISH TRIPLETS FOR CHRISTMAS

Available now from Love Inspired!

*Find more great reads at
www.LoveInspired.com*

Dear Reader,

Thank you for following Anna and Fletcher on their sometimes rocky, sometimes smooth trip down memory lane and back again.

Although their story is fictional, it was loosely inspired by my experiences observing loved ones suffering from head injuries and memory loss, the effects of which were frightening and frustrating for everyone involved. It's such a relief to know we can trust the Lord for comfort, guidance and healing during those situations.

Trust also plays a vital role in falling in love. Remember when you first risked sharing your heart with that special person in your life? Remember when that special person began opening up to you? As Dr. Donovan told Anna and Fletcher, falling in love is a gift. It's something to celebrate. Fortunately, we don't need to suffer amnesia to relive that joy: we can experience it by calling our memories to mind.

May all your romantic relationships have more songs than stones!

Blessings,
Carrie Lighte

Get 2 Free Books,
Plus 2 Free Gifts—
just for trying the Reader Service!